Con

Coma Dreams

and Other Stories

Gary Springer

Coma Dreams

For Reid and Jesus,
Kings of Men

Joe

"Fuckers threw bricks at me," Joe said. He wiped blood from his ear, walked to one side of my apartment, shifted his grip on his hammer, then walked to the other.

"I had one of them punks," he said. "Had him cold. Had him down in the grass. Then his buddies started with the bricks."

I asked Joe more questions, but he couldn't hear me. He paced the floor mumbling about what he was going to do to the punk kids when he caught them.

"Get dressed," he said. "We're getting my bike back."

Joe wasn't big. He weighed less than one-fifty. He wasn't tall, either. Maybe five-nine, five-ten with his workboots on. At a glance he could pass for a man in his thirties. A closer look revealed the white hairs in his beard, the silver streaks among his black and tangled dreadlocks, the permanent weariness he carried in his legs.

Joe grew up on the streets of south Philly. As a kid, he boxed in the gym of the legendary Joe Frazier. He won most of his amateur fights, considered turning pro, then ended up in the Marines. He served a couple tours then got out. Back in Philly, he didn't find anything but trouble. One guy broke the fat end of a poolstick over his head in a barfight. Another took a shovel to his face in an alley. The poolstick laid him out cold and damaged his memory for life. The shovel left a three-inch scar down his cheek that still opened up twenty years later.

We walked to my car under a half-moon sky. I thought some nicotine might cool him down so I handed him a cigarette from a pack in glovebox.

"We can't drive," I said. "My starter went out this morning."

Joe paused before striking the match. He absorbed the news like one more blow to the face, one more burden on his back.

"Then we're walking," he said.

We headed down Colonial Avenue into the heart of town. Joe turned his head to follow every passing biker.

"Your ear alright, Joe?"

He gave a quick, flicking nod of his head. "Fine."

We passed a block of restaurants and coffeeshops. Most were closed. We passed a slew of bars, banks, and grocery stores. No bikes, no kids.

We stopped beneath a streetlight at the edge of a new block.

"You want to turn back, Joe?"

Joe didn't answer. His eyes scanned the streets in all directions.

I dug the pack from my pocket and lit another cigarette. When I held the pack out to Joe, he was gone.

I spotted him halfway down the block. Beyond him, I saw a biker.

I tossed my cigarette and joined the chase. I was younger but Joe was faster. His old legs pounded their anger against the pavement. He made a strong push, came within arm's reach of the biker, then stopped suddenly.

After a dozen strides, I caught up to him. "Is that your bike, Joe?"

"Right color," he said, "wrong bike."

As we caught our breath, the biker braked. He put one leg on the ground and looked back at us. "What the hell?" he said.

"Everything's cool," I said.

"Fuck you everything's cool," the biker said.

"Our bad," I said. "We thought you were someone else."

The biker pushed his bike toward us. He pointed at the hammer inside Joe's jacket. "Everything ain't cool," he said. "I see the axe."

Joe ignored the biker. He looked up and down the block.

The biker rested his hands on the handlebars. Moonlight flickered across gold and silver rings on his fingers. He was scrawny. He had long, greasy hair and a wispy moustache.

"Everything's cool," I said. "We thought you had his bike."

The biker's expression changed. The forced toughness turned sly. He held his hand out to Joe. "That's aright," he said. "What's up, bro?"

Joe looked down at the hand like it was leprous. He nudged it away with his forearm. The biker shrugged and turned to me. I shook his hand. The biker smiled and reached into his pocket. In a gesture supposed to be teasing, he inched a plastic bag out of the pocket. "You guys lookin?"

"Like I got money for that," Joe said.

The biker pushed his lips out slowly and shook his head. "Colombian white, bro. Candy for the black man."

"Fuck off," Joe said.

We left the biker. Joe led the way back to the bars and coffeeshops without talking.

We stopped at a bus-stop bench, lit fresh cigarettes, and watched the cars drive by. Joe leaned back, weary. He took half-hearted pulls from his smoke. From his face I could see that the anger and adrenalen were gone. Tomorrow's burdens were beginning to weigh on him.

"How'm I gonna get around now?" he said. "How'm I gonna get work?"

Joe didn't have a regular job. He biked all over town in search of construction crews that might take on an extra hand. The big crews hired only trained and licensed workers. The small crews were more lax. They didn't ask questions and paid cash under-the-table. Trouble was, any boss willing to hire someone off the street was just as likely to skip work hungover or stiff his employees on payday.

"Now I gotta walk," Joe said. "Walk ten miles a day just to hear someone tell me no."

"We'll find your bike," I said. "I can give you rides once my car gets fixed."

"No, you got your own work to do." He tossed his cigarette and stood up slowly. "Go get some rest," he said. "I'll see you tomorrow."

"You going home?"

He shook his head, felt the hammer inside his jacket, and headed down the street.

A Little Candy

Everyone has to survive. You do what you have to. Salesmen unbalance the truth. Inmates stab their enemies so they don't get stabbed themselves. Waitresses flirt with men they don't really like for a few extra dollars. You do what you have to. Everyone does it.

He put in a solid forty each week. If they needed overtime, he stayed late without complaint. He worked hard for a boss who didn't care, alongside co-workers who wouldn't stop if they saw him broken down on the side of the road. When he got home at night, he needed some entertainment. He liked a good baseball game. He liked war movies and wrestling. With a full stomach and a cold beer in his hand, he liked to watch the girls dance on the Spanish channel.

Mornings were hard. Every time the alarm buzzed he had to find a reason to get up. As a young man he had used hope and ambition, but the man rounding thirty knew the value of shrewdness. He used little pleasures, little candies, to summon the strength to rise from his bed. He teased himself with visions of Spanish breasts. He baited himself with the smell of scrambled eggs and the taste of his first cigarette.

Days were just as hard. When the morning hours dragged, he thought about where he was going to eat for lunch. When the afternoon dragged, he thought about the television shows that would be on that night.

Was his life sad? Maybe. He'd seen worse. Some of the guys he'd grown up with had sprayed their kids across the old neighborhood like come across tile. The fighters that had walked the high-school halls so proudly now filled jail cells or wandered the streets for drugs. The divorced ones limped through life with broken hearts. The few still married would have been better off alone.

Happiness is for the young and the selfish, he said to himself in the sleepless hours of the night. I don't ask life for much. Just give me a little candy and I'll get by.

Broken Fingers

Darren was a player. Women and basketball. He told the country girl he loved her the night before she moved away. He promised to write. He left her shivering in the bed.

Paul was a wrestler, as country as his big sister. He swallowed his parents' divorce without saying a word. His sister went to live with their father, Paul chose their mother.

In the heart of the basketball season, when Darren's shots couldn't miss and the whole world seemed his fan, he found Paul waiting for him outside the gym.

How much is a broken heart worth? Paul asked. How much is my sister worth?

Darren shrugged. Don't know what you're talking about.

Paul took Darren by the hand and broke his finger.

Darren's shots still sank game after game. He finished the season as hot as he began it. He found Paul waiting for him outside the locker room after his last game.

You still ain't done what's right, Paul said.

Paul broke another finger.

A few days later some of Darren's friends cornered Paul behind the cafeteria.

You're done with Darren, they said. No more broken fingers. You got it?

Paul knocked the hand off his chest. He shook his head. It's done when he does right.

Darren couldn't sleep. He hated Paul. He lay in bed thinking about the way Paul walked and talked, his thick bulldog neck, his stupid cowboy hat with the feather in front. He imagined fighting him, stunning him with jabs, knocking him to his knees with a huge right hand.

Instead he wrote a letter for Paul's sister.

Paul read the letter. Shaking his head, he handed the letter back to Darren.

You still don't get it, he said. You're scared, but you're only thinking about yourself.

Darren pulled his hands away. He clenched his fists, ready to fight.

Paul walked away.

Two years later, in a musty country church with eight pine pews and a secondhand organ, Paul heard his uncle preach about Zacchaeus, the little man that climbed a tree to see Jesus. His uncle said that Jesus walks into the life of every person just like he did for little Zacchaeus. He said that if you're not ready, if you don't climb that tree when you've got the chance, you might never see Jesus again.

Paul got scared. At the end of the service he walked to the front of the church, got down on his knees, and gave his life to the Lord.

Paul graduated from high-school and headed to college. He was a new man but something never felt right inside him. The answer came one night as he bowed his bulldog neck in prayer.

Paul found Darren at his fraternity on a Saturday night.

The two faced each other in the middle of the yard. Paul stood alone, Darren with a circle of brothers behind him.

I'm sorry about your finger, Paul said. I shouldn't have done what I did.

Fingers, Darren said. Fingers.

I'm sorry for breaking your fingers, Paul said. He cocked his head to the side a little and squinted as he thought for a moment. You might have deserved one finger, he said, but not two.

So you're only sorry for breaking one of my fingers?

You did a mean and terrible thing, Darren. Maybe I wasn't the guy to do the breaking, though.

Darren grinned at Paul. He grinned at his brothers and they grinned back.

In the last three years Darren had also been through changes. When he first got to college, he quickly discovered that he wasn't the best-looking guy around anymore. He wasn't the richest in his fraternity, the best dressed, or even the best basketball player. For the first time in his life he was just another guy.

Being just another guy wasn't something Darren could accept. He drifted along, sullen and depressed, until his opportunity came. On a drunken Friday night he crossed paths with a member of a rival fraternity under a streetlight. They exchanged words. Darren was drunk but the other guy could barely stand. Darren grinned before knocking the guy out with a punch he never saw coming.

Next morning, when the brothers sat around telling stories of their conquests the previous night, Darren bragged about his knockout. No one believed him. On Monday, though, the guy was seen on campus with his jaw wired shut.

Darren boosted his reputation with another knockout the following weekend, his victim again a stumbling drunk. Hooked on the rush, fueled by his brothers' fear and respect, he kept on fighting. He avoided guys he couldn't take, destroyed those he could. He was slow to talk, but quick to punch. He learned the exact postures and expressions that could get a man to lower his guard. Darren became a badass, a cheapshot, a coward.

His brothers loved the feeling they got whenever they saw that look in Darren's eye.

They felt it now as Darren shrugged and extended his hand to Paul.

Paul accepted the hand. He shook it firmly and gave a nod of respect.

When the hand pulled Paul closer, he was confused. He watched Darren's forehead lurch forehead. He felt the plate of thick bone crash into his nose, shatter it, send a riot of tremors through his head and spine. His legs lost all strength. He fell to one knee.

Darren stepped back to survey the damage he had done. He watched the gush of blood flow freely down Paul's face and soak his shirt. He heard his brothers cheering, laughing. They patted his shoulders, but he pushed them away and walked to Paul.

He stood over him. He pulled him up by the arm. The two faced each other again in the middle of the yard.

Darren held two fingers in front of Paul's face. He turned them to show their wicked, unnatural bend.

Are we finished? he said.

Paul wiped his mouth. He tilted his head back, swallowed some blood, then spit in the grass.

Yeah, we're finished.

Darren held out his hand. Paul shook it.

This time Paul was the one that pulled Darren closer. They touched cheeks as Paul whispered into Darren's ear.

Justice. Truth. Punishment. They're too heavy for a good man to carry. How is a guy like you going to do it?

Trudy's Colors

Trudy paints. Some kids play ball. Some kids watch TV. Some kids beat other kids. My girl paints.

When she was four, she said that God was stingy. I asked her why. She said that God made the world too big to paint. How you gonna paint a mountain, she asked? You gonna dip it in the ocean? You gonna make a raincloud to sprinkle red on it? No, God was stingy, she said, swinging her head from side to side to show that we were finished talking about it.

Sun don't shine where we live. Too much brick up high. Rain falls on you now and again to remind you that there's a sky. Cars honk to never let you forget that there's a ground. And me and Trudy just hang in the middle. When I ain't sweating under a Pontiac with oil on my face or sweating on the blacktop shooting ball, I watch her paint. She says she paints for her only Daddy in the whole world. She must have done ten dozen pictures of me alone. I kept em all but told her to go on to other stuff. She tried to paint her Mama once, too. Used all her imagination for this pretty picture of a lady with orange hair and skinny little brown arms. That ain't your Mama, I said, and that was that.

I used to get Trudy's paint for her. Had to go at night cause my days are owned by the shop. Problem was nobody liked a black man on their fire escape at two after midnight no matter what he said he was doing. So now I let her go during the day with that punk Roffi. Roffi likes her stuff so he don't hurt her none. Somebody yells at her, Roffi yells back. Somebody comes at her, Roffi steps up. She comes back with her garbage bag full of all kinds of colors. Then me and Roffi just watch.

She doesn't know we're there once she starts painting. She

spreads the newspapers in front of her, two pages if she's really feeling it, dumps all the broken chips of paint in a mound, then starts sorting them into little paint piles. Roffi don't know and neither do I how she sorts them. Not by color, cause I seen her put a white chip from the window sill with muddy flakes of rust from the roof. Not by place, cause I seen her put a white chip from the same window with a chip from the fire hydrant. Not by size, either. Best we know, it's touch. Trudy can tell just by touching a piece where it belongs.

So she sorts them into piles and then she paints, maybe using a little water or milk to make the paints run better. Colors make a picture, she says, nothing else. It ain't what you paint or how you paint, it's the colors you use. You got to see your own rainbow in the sky, she says, not the one that God put up there. That ain't just talk, either, cause I seen my girl make a rainbow out of rust and an angel's face out of dirt.

Thing is with most of Trudy's stuff, and even Roffi can tell you this, at first glance you don't know what it is. But you feel it. Something on that flat page grabs you and you don't notice that's it almost all dirt brown. Something grabs you, like Trudy knew what you was dreaming about last night and set it down on paper. You take a step closer and you're lost in it. You look left to right and you see a city busting apart. You look up and down and you see the face of a little boy crying. Then you just sit and stare and let it take you. Cause Trudy can. Trudy can take you anywhere.

She don't know but I got it all. Everything she ever painted right there in my closet in one big stack of old newspapers. I can't put them anywhere else since she hates seeing her own stuff once she's done. She says it feels like the picture dies after her hand leaves the paper. Not to me it don't. I still got her first picture of me. I keep it under my bed, folded perfect between two old phone books. Every now and then, when the world's beat me good and my head's saying I'm nothing, I grab the phone books, pull out my picture, and unfold it slow as my big old hands can manage. Just one look and I'm better cause in that picture I see how my little girl sees me and that's enough to get me by.

Teacher once called me in. She said that my girl should go to a special school for special artists. Her and this skinny guy took me and Trudy to visit the school. The place had everything: marble halls, a thousand paintings, busted-up statues of naked people, clean toilets. Teacher said that with a little time and schooling they could make my girl into a great painter, a master, like all these old foreign guys she couldn't stop talking about. I thought about it a while, with Trudy tugging on my arm and begging the whole time, till a vision came to my head. I saw my little girl sitting down on a marble floor, painting on the purest white paper with a real wooden brush in her hand and a million jars of colors at her feet. A crowd of people were looking over her shoulder, but not me. Vision didn't have me anywhere.

So I told the teacher no. I said that nobody could teach Trudy to become great because she already was. I said that if they made Trudy into a master then she wouldn't be Trudy anymore.

We went home. I watched my little girl cry till I thought it was me that was dying. I went to the fire escape and I looked up at the sky of bricks and I yelled at the God that had made Trudy's world so damn big. I yelled at him and I cussed him good cause he knew Trudy before I did and he still made her the way she is. And he made me, too. And as long as my girl sees rainbows she ain't gonna paint for nobody else but me.

Scott

I found Scott sleeping in the back of a pickup truck under a mound of wet, ratty blankets on a cold November morning. He looked up at me with a single bloodshot eye.

"How ya doin?" I said.

"Been better," he said.

"You didn't spend the night out here, did you?"

He nodded. The blankets shook free from his head. He had old man's skin, a three-week beard, and thick, brown hair. His nose, obviously broken a time or two, was wide at the bridge and bulbed at the end.

I tapped frost from an overhanging tree branch. "You must be freezing," I said.

"Might have pneumonia," he said with a cough.

"You don't have anywhere to go?"

"This is my friend's truck. He doesn't mind."

"No house or apartment, though? No family or anything?"

He coughed again, shook his head, then burrowed back under his blankets.

"Come on up," I said. "You can stay at my place for a while."

He sat on my couch for an hour without saying much. Beneath some dry blankets the shivering gradually worked its way out of his shoulders and legs. His hands kept shaking, though.

"I'm not going to lie to you," he said. "I'm an alcoholic."

"You can't get drunk here."

"I won't. I just have to sip. If I don't, the shakes get worse."

I watched the violent twitch and flutter of his fingers. His hands appeared on the verge of seizure.

"I can go," he said. "If you don't want me here, I'll leave. Just say the word."

"Where else are you gonna go?"

He shrugged. He pulled his hands under the blankets and stared at the floor.

"That's alright," I said. "You can stay."

"I also gotta tell straight out, right up front that I was in prison," he said. "Eighteen years. Florida State."

"What for?"

"Murder."

I studied Scott's eyes and wondered if he was bullshitting me. Why would he hurt his chances of having a warm place to stay?

"You really killed somebody?"

"Yes, sir, I did."

"Why?"

"Guy stole from me," he said. "I was a stupid kid back then. Just a crazy kid."

Scott looked at least fifty years old, probably sixty. His face was sad, his body sickly. Maybe he had killed a man once, but now he was beaten down and broken.

"Let's get you some food," I said.

We drove to the grocery store. As he got out of his seat, I noticed that his legs gave him a lot of trouble. He hobbled across the parking lot with a stiff-kneed limp.

"Lady hit me," he said. "Ran me down over on Del Mar. Shattered the left leg in four places, the right in six. They had to put in metal rods."

"You look like you're going to fall," I said.

"I'm alright," he said. "The knees lock up sometimes."

I slowed down to match his wobbly stride as we walked the aisles of the store. Occasionally, I reached out a hand to steady him. His flannel shirt was grimy to the touch. Its blue fabric had stained to black, and its white to grey. I expected him to stink, but his smell was strangely, sickly sweet, a mix of fruit and sweat and alcohol.

He drew stares from the people passing by. I was embarrassed at being seen with him, but I also felt an odd sense of pride. Scott had an intensity, an aura, unlike anyone else I had known. Though he could barely stand, he managed to swagger. Though weak and ill, his thin frame carried an air of violence, not the immediate threat of violence, more the raw history of violence carved upon his body.

We grabbed some white bread, peanut butter, jelly, and two 40s of malt liquor.

For the next week Scott stayed at my place during the day while I went to work. When I got home at night, I always found him in the same spot on the couch, curled up in his blankets, shivering, sipping his warm 40, watching TV. I checked my things when he went to the bathroom but never found anything missing.

We smoked on the fire escape at night. Most of the time, I asked questions and he told stories.

"So what did the guy steal from you anyway?" I asked.

"My wrench," he said.

"You killed a guy over a wrench?"

"He was a punk. He'd been stealing my tools for weeks. When I saw my best wrench gone, I left the garage, walked straight to his apartment, and kicked in the door. Caught him right in the middle of riding his girlfriend. I looked him in the eye, shot him in the head, and took back my wrench." Scott paused to grind his cigarette into the bottom of the coffee can. "I warned him. I told him I was gonna do it. I told him the next time he touched my stuff I'd put a bullet in his head. Sure enough, I did."

I imagined a younger Scott storming into a dark, sweaty apartment. I saw the thief's face, his look of pleasure turned to terror, saw the young girl scream, push the naked body off, saw Scott kick through the clothes on the floor looking for his wrench. "Did you hurt the girl?" I asked.

"Hell, no. I never hurt a woman in my life."

"What about the guy? Do you regret killing him?"

Scott stared into the dark sky for a moment then shook his head. "I warned him."

From his stories I pieced together the general course, or rather descent, of his life. He got kicked out of school in sixth-grade for throwing a chair at his teacher. He spent most of his early teens in juvenile halls. His parents kicked him out of the house at sixteen. By eighteen, he was pulling armed robberies up and down the east coast. By twenty-three he was in Florida State.

He had two brothers. He hadn't spoken to them in years and didn't know where they lived anymore. He had a sister in Houston, but he dismissed her as being too religious. He talked casually about the passing of his mother. Only the memories of his father drew any emotion from him. He spoke about the beatings his father had given him with a strange mixture of hatred and respect.

"Did they ever catch you on the armed robberies?" I asked.

"Not once," he said with pride. "That doesn't mean we always got the money, though. There was this one old bastard at a grocery store in Carolina. I showed him my gun and he just shook his head. 'Give me the money, old man,' I said. 'I ain't giving you shit,' he said."

"What did you do?"

"I told him I guess I had the wrong store."

Scott told me stories about prison, too. Sometimes he told me more than I wanted to know.

"I got my share of ass in prison," he bragged one night.

I thought about cutting him off, but a perverse curiosity kept me quiet.

"I controlled all the drug money in my block," he said. "Guys would do about anything I wanted." After a pause, he added, "Don't worry, man. I'm not gay. It was just something to do, you know. Prison ain't a good place to be."

He told me how they made weapons out of sharpened comb handles, dried-up soap, even rolled-up magazines. He told me about the fresh sweetleaf tobacco they chewed when they worked in the fields.

During his second weekend at my place, he had an attack of emphysema. He turned pale and broke out in a sweat. When his breathing got desperate, I drove him to the hospital.

After a two-hour wait in the ER, the nurse led us back to the examining room. She tossed a gown onto Scott's bed, gave him a cold glance, then moved on to the patient next to him. Scott stripped without closing the curtain. His upper body revealed more green-black prison ink than bare skin. Eight-balls, snakes, skulls, racecars, and revolvers filled his arms and chest. He lay down on the bed, closed his eyes, and tried to breathe. He looked scared.

After another hour of waiting, I got bored. "I've got some work to do," I said. "I'll come back later." Scott nodded without opening his eyes.

I cleaned my apartment until midnight then drove back toward the hospital. On the way there I stopped at a gas station for cigarettes. I saw something odd as I walked out of the station: a clean, well-dressed woman pushing a shopping cart stuffed with clothes.

Curious, I lit a cigarette and met her at the corner.

"How's it going?" I asked.

She tapped the crosswalk button three or four times. "Pretty bad, actually," she said.

"I'm sorry."

She looked me over, trying to gage my motives for approaching her. "Can I have a smoke?" she asked.

"Sure."

She lit the cigarette, leaned against the shopping cart, and stared down the street. The light changed, but she didn't move.

"I just lost my apartment," she said. "Lost my job two weeks ago. Lost my apartment tonight. I walked all the way to the mission, but they wouldn't take me."

"Why not?"

"Believe it or not, they only accept substance abusers."

"What if you're homeless, though?"

"You have to be a homeless alcoholic or a homeless drug addict."

"That makes no sense," I said. "Where are you headed now?"

"I'm not sure. I'm going to try to call my cousin again. I heard about another shelter downtown that might take me."

"That's a hell of a walk. You want a ride?"

"I'm alright."

"It's no problem."

"Are you sure?"

"Yeah. Just let me call the hospital to check on my friend."

She walked with me to a payphone on the side of the gas station. I called the hospital and found Scott after a few transfers.

"How long are they gonna keep you?" I asked.

"Another hour or so," Scott said. His breathing sounded much better. "They got me on oxygen."

"That's good. I'm gonna give somebody a ride and then come back to pick you up."

"Who is it?"

"Just a lady I met on the street. She got kicked out of her apartment and needs a ride to a shelter."

"Is she black?"

"Yeah, she's black. So what?"

"Don't do it, man."

"Why not?"

"It's a sucker move. She's going to lead you into the middle of nowhere and let her niggers jump you. They'll beat you good and steal your car."

"I don't think so, Scott. I was the one that approached her."

"It's a sucker move, man. Mark my words."

"I'll be fine," I said. "I'll be at the hospital in a half-hour."

Scott mumbled something then hung up.

I stepped back and let the woman use the phone. I thought about Scott's warning as she dialed.

She spoke to someone for a couple minutes then hung up.

"My cousin's coming to get me," she said, smiling with relief. "Thanks for the offer, though."

Scott quit sipping in the third week. He graduated from one forty a day to two or three.

In the middle of the week, I noticed that my TV had been turned upside down. I saw long cracks down both its sides.

I found Scott smoking on the fire escape.

"What the hell happened to my TV, Scott?" I said.

He gave me a confused, quizzical look. "What are you talking about?"

"Come here."

He tossed his cigarette, limped down the stairs, and followed me into the apartment. When he saw the cracks in the TV, he took a quick step back.

"It's cracked," he said.

"Yeah, I know it's cracked," I said. "It's upside-down, too. What the hell did you do?"

He glanced at me then back at the TV. He took a long, heavy breath and wobbled to the side.

"Alright," he said. "I'm a man. I admit it. I bumped your TV."

"How did you do that?"

"I was coming out of the kitchen and my leg gave out. The knee locked up, you know. It's the metal rods."

"It's not the fucking rods," I said, "it's the beer."

I plugged in the TV and pressed the power. Miraculously, a clear picture of an upside-down basketball game appeared.

"We need to talk," I said. "Let's go for a walk."

We walked a few blocks to a quiet neighborhood. We sat down on the curb.

"What are you going to do for the rest of your life, Scott?"

"I'm just trying to survive," he said. "That's all I've ever done."

"You should get a job. Maybe work on cars again."

"I can't. Not with these legs."

"You gotta do something, Scott. It's no good the way you're living."

"I get six-hundred a month disability. That's enough for us to split a two-bedroom. If I had my own room, I wouldn't be in your way all the time."

"That's not the problem. The problem is the alcohol."

"I've been drinking for fifty years. I can't stop now."

"You have to stop."

Scott started to say something, but his voice choked up. He looked away.

"You have to find a source of strength," I said. "What's the most important thing in the world to you?"

His mouth opened as he thought about the question. While I waited, I lit a cigarette. I offered him one, but he didn't seem to see it.

"I was married once," he said. "Greatest woman in the world. We were together for twelve years."

"What was she like?"

"Sweet, pure, kind, loving."

"What happened?"

"One day I found her sitting in the car. She had the keys in her hand, but she couldn't figure out what to do with them. I watched her stare at the steering wheel for twenty minutes."

"Alzheimer's?"

He nodded. "She never hurt anybody in her life. Never said an unkind word to me in twelve years. By the end, she couldn't even feed herself. Never forgot how to fuck, though. She loved doing that till the day she died."

From Scott's face I could tell that his wife had been the brightest part of his life. He really loved her. Her memory might be the only thing that could save him.

"What do you think she would say if she was here?"

"I don't know."

"Do you think she'd like the way you're living?"

"She never told me what to do. She just wanted me to be happy."

Scott kept himself to one forty a day until the weekend. He

broke on Sunday. When I got back from a movie, I found him curled up on the floor in only his underwear, an empty vodka bottle by his head. Except for the butterknife in his hand, he looked like a giant, sleeping, tattooed baby.

He blinked his bleary eyes four or five times after I turned the light on. When his eyes finally focused, he stabbed at my legs with the butterknife. He missed by three feet, but continued to stab. He pawed through the air with a pathetic maliciousness.

"Scott, what are you doing?"

He held the knife at his chest, blinked a few times, coughed, then started stabbing again.

"Scott, what the hell are you doing?"

This time he looked up from the ground. He stared at my face for several seconds.

"Protecting your shit," he said. He clutched the knife to his chest and rolled away from me.

The next morning I kicked him awake at seven.

"You're gone, dude."

"What?"

"I said you're gone. I'm taking you to the mission."

"Can I go tonight?"

"You're going now."

Scott was still stumbling-drunk. He fell down hard in the mission parking lot. His elbows struck the concrete and came up bloody. As I helped him to the front office, I noticed the stares of the men inside the fence. They looked at Scott with contempt. Maybe his lowly condition reminded them of the low places they had been. Maybe, being bullshitters themselves, they saw through Scott's bullshit in a glance.

A year later, I saw him on the street. He had giant, purple-black bruises under both his eyes. He looked like a grotesque raccoon. We met on the sidewalk and shook hands. I asked how he was doing. He told a long, rambling story about the park, punk kids, and boobytraps.

The Last Tour

*Before the Prophet came, the tour was filled with all kinds: ex-*military too wild for the office world, ex-bouncers awaiting trial for getting too rough with their customers, ex-cons fresh from prison weight rooms, ex-waitresses tired of getting groped at work and home, ex-athletes looking for one last show, one last trail of glory.

The tour never stopped. It wound and snaked its way across North America year to year, season to season, town to town. In the winter it dipped into the southern states, the desert towns of Arizona and Nevada, even Sonora and Coahuila, Mexico. In the summer it headed to the northwest states, some provinces of Canada, even Alaska. The tour picked up new recruits in each city at local bars, hotels, and restaurants, then lost a few to local jails.

A battered Greyhound served as flagship of the tour. The driver, a retired wrestler himself, kept the bus running through daily miracles of improvised repairs. In bad times the bus plodded over mountains and rivers alone. In good times small caravans followed the bus, pickups with breast-flashing groupies, vans stuffed with costumes, cars filled with fearless young men eager for their first moment in the ring.

Most wrestlers stayed on for two or three months, maybe a year. Those that avoided neck and back injuries were usually done in by the slim and sporadic paydays. They stayed with the tour until it wound its way back to their hometown then jumped ship. Doctors lasted a year or two, wardrobe and equipment people about the same. Managers were the most unpredictable. Honest ones lasted years and boosted the reputation of the tour from coast to coast. Dishonest ones stole the purse and disappeared in the night. Teddy, the busdriver, watched the young faces come and go every year. No one knew how long he'd been on the tour. Some said decades.

The Prophet snuck onto the tour somewhere in Oregon. He hauled equipment for a few shows then worked his way backstage. With surprising speed he immersed himself in every aspect of the show and gained the wrestlers' trust. He patched them up after brutal matches. He gave them valuable suggestions to improve their costume and character. The villains and heels became more hated, the heroes more beloved. Though he was skinny as a rail, he demonstrated new moves for the wrestlers and refined their old ones.

The tour prospered. Wrestlers still came and went with the wind, but a fresh spirit was emerging. Everyone on the crew felt it. They stopped their backstage bickering and began to encourage and support each other. They took pride in their individual roles, no matter how menial or unseen. Everyone sensed that something special was happening, maybe the dawning of a golden age.

Audiences responded. The crowds felt that they were watching something vibrant and spontaneous, not scripted. They saw real anger on the wrestlers' faces, real pain, fear, lust, and betrayal. Wrestlers left everything in the ring and the crowds roared.

But the Devil struck in Bakersfield. Avalanche overdosed on painkillers in his dressing room; Lolita found out she was pregnant, father unknown; and the Egyptian Conniption broke his collarbone on his way through a table.

In the chaos after the show, the manager stole the purse and split town.

An angry mob gathered around the bus at midnight demanding to be paid. Teddy locked the bus doors. He lit a cigar, rested his feet on the console, and waved at the furious wrestlers.

The chaos grew.

The Farm Boys argued with Team Turquoise then suddenly

broke into a brawl among themselves. Before the Farm Boys could be separated, Lolita grabbed Corrie Spade by the hair, lifted her into the air, and bounced her head off the hood of an SUV.

Suddenly, the chaos became more chaotic. Within seconds every person in the parking lot was involved. Wardrobe people choked roadies. Trainers clubbed doctors. Midgets jumped from the hoods of cars. The entire parking lot became a medieval battleground.

In the midst of the madness, the Prophet climbed onto the top of the bus. He gazed across the crowd with a heavy sadness in his eyes then lifted the megaphone to his lips.

"Friends," he said, "listen to me."

His voice echoed against the stadium wall. It returned twice as loud. Some of the brawlers stopped fighting and turned to listen. Others continued to deliver or receive their beatings.

"Friends," the Prophet shouted, "I can save wrestling!"

All of the brawlers stopped. A tense and thin quietness spread over the crowd. They held their clenched fists in check as they looked to the top of the bus. The bus door slid open. Teddy stepped out. He spit, tossed his cigar onto the pavement, then squinted as he looked up.

The Prophet made a sweeping gesture over the crowd with his bony arm.

"This isn't wrestling, my friends," he said. "Wrestling isn't about money and muscles and violence. Wrestling is about morality and courage and violence. It's about good and evil. Good and evil must clash. You wrestlers are the timeless symbols of that beautiful collision. You are athletes and actors and artists. You are the luckiest people on earth."

"You don't know wrestling," Jojo Tambori said. "I could break you in half."

"I do know wrestling, Jojo. I love wrestling. I'm a man of vision who has seen the future. I know the future of wrestling because I've studied its past." The Prophet pointed at Teddy. "Do you know who that man is?"

"Yeah, he's the busdriver," Jojo said.

The Prophet shook his head sadly. "He's not a busdriver, Jojo. That great man is walking history. In 1957, he ended Thad the Impaler's three-year reign of terror with a sleeperhold that could have snapped a bull's neck. In 1962, he single-handedly defeated the Asphalt Warriors—Benny, Ted, and Jay—in a ninety-minute war in Tallahassee. After President Kennedy was shot, he and Randolph Valentino beat each other beyond recognition to help the people of Knoxville forget their pain, if only for a moment. We've lost our way, my friends."

The Prophet nodded at Teddy. The old man saluted.

"When I was seven years old," the Prophet continued," my parents took my sister and me to our first show. It was the 16th of August, 1961. Dizzy from the heat and our own excitement, we sat in the back of our Chevy Impala for five long hours over the backroads of Wyoming. After the first match, my father turned to me and said, 'Son, it was worth the trip.' After the last match, my sister cried. I asked her what was wrong and she said, 'The mean man submitted the Prince. The mean man won.' My friends, that is the power of wrestling."

Jojo Tambori dipped his head for a moment. He looked around at his fellow wrestlers then up to the Prophet.

"We've lost our way," Jojo said. "What can we do now?"

"Follow me," the Prophet said.

The Bitter Faithful

She thought about pain sometimes, she thought about death.
Pain was a showman. It struck the nerves with fire then pulled
back and listened to the cries. It watched with pride the wild
twisting of the body, the desperate eyes and breath, the hopeless
attempts to escape one's own skin. Death needed no show. It
crushed with a shadow, consumed with a whisper.

Who was she to question? What did she know about pain
or death? Her father was the body in the bed. He was the one
that groaned, shook, and twisted as he resisted the disease night
and day. She watched him fight, eyes closed, teeth grinding.
When the disease rested, she watched him draw his breath in
careful fragments while he waited for the next wave of pain.

He hadn't known pain until his middle years. When he had
rounded forty, his back and joints had deteriorated under the
strain from a lifetime of building trusses. In his fifties he had
experienced a host of minor ailments: infections of the small
organs cured with a couple weeks of antibiotics, faulty glands
that confused the body's delicate messenger system, recurring
pneumonia and bronchitis. He had endured the ailments with a
sense of humor, reflexive and forced. "I can't complain," he said
to his daughter over quiet, Italian dinners. "It's not half as bad
as what your mother did to me."

In his sixties the death of his second wife had ushered in
the heavyweights. His kidneys had faltered. Cancer had taken
his colon and prostate then settled deep inside his lungs. His
hope had withered. She watched the man once strong in body
and spirit, once invincible in the eyes of a little girl, become
bedridden.

While her brothers and sisters delivered their love in greeting cards and Sunday phone calls, she took care of him. She cooked her best meals for him then watched the plates sit untouched at the side of his bed. She changed his sheets twice a day, washed the filth from his body, and fetched juice at the first sound of cracking in his throat. Her own health suffered but she never complained. (How could you complain about a little exhaustion and some migraines when someone else was dying?) When she thought she couldn't take anymore, she smoked a cigarette deep in the garden or popped a few mother's little helpers.

On rare, clear nights they sat together on the patio and watched the twilight fill the trees and garden. He spoke with calm on these nights. He shared with her his many regrets and his sweetest memories. She told him that he had been a great father, the best.

His mind left him before the end. To her this was the greatest blow of all. She watched his fevered eyes pass over her without recognition. She could have been a plant to him, a pillow. He mumbled streams of nonsense like an infant at play with the language of his parents. Eventually, his tongue thickened and he spoke no words at all. He shriveled to bones under the final seal of cancer.

Her brothers and sisters wept at the funeral. They spoke kind words about their father to those gathered. They hugged their sister, praised her devotion, then filed uneasily past the casket.

She stared at the casket until the cathedral emptied.

Her son and daughter kissed her dry cheeks then waited outside.

Her husband touched her shoulder. "Are you ready?"

She turned to him. She stared long into his face. Was this man with the dark and tired eyes her husband? He could be a stranger. She crossed the chasm of years and remembered their early love, the nights together. She remembered the light of his skin, the way he whispered, the arms so strong she thought they could hold back all the pain and sorrow in the world.

"You're helpless," she said. "You're just a man and you're helpless."

A puff of air escaped his mouth. His tired eyes sharpened. He walked away, left her alone in the church.

Her eyes returned to the casket.

Some time later she kissed her father. She touched the casket, felt the firmness of the oak.

(a passage from HereAfter, unpublished)

Uncle Peter was my favorite uncle. He was a preacher in a small farmtown where most of the working men saw preaching as just an excuse to get out of real work. Despite the deep-rooted attitudes against him, Peter worked hard at what he did. He lived on next to nothing. He cared for the people of his congregation like doctors are meant to care for their patients.

He was a great preacher but a terrible farmer. In the summer my dad sent me to Peter's ten-acre farm to help out for a few weeks. We tried different projects—fencing, roofing, painting, irrigation—with varying degrees of success and occasional injuries.

The workday started with breakfast in the predawn darkness and continued until the noonday sun made the tools too hot to hold. Aunt Carol fed me like a king since they couldn't afford to pay me. For breakfast we had eggs, bacon, coffee, a mound of hashbrowns, and a stack of toast. For lunch we had roast beef, corn-on-the-cob, mashed potatoes and gravy, biscuits and honey, steamed carrots, and a pitcher of water for each of us.

When the lunch settled into our stomachs, we took a nap on the side of the house under the shade of the sycamores. The stream carried us to sleep with its rocky gurgling and kept us cool with its misty breezes. My uncle loved to talk when he woke up. We started conversations about all kinds of things, but usually ended up talking about God. Uncle Peter wasn't pushy with his ideas and he listened as much as talked so I didn't really mind.

During those sleepy conversations I learned about my family history. I heard stories about my grandmother that died from stomach cancer before I was born, my alcoholic great-grandfather that disappeared into the big-city streets, my cousin in prison for manslaughter. I also heard how Uncle Peter and Aunt Carol had fallen in love their first year of college.

Before he would start a story about my dad, he would look up into the trees, shake his head, and smile. He told the stories like he was still struggling to believe them.

"Your dad was wild."

"My dad?"

"Believe it or not, your dad was crazy. Everybody worried about him, especially your grandmother. He had this nasty, souped-up dirtbike that he rode all over the country. I hated the sound of that thing. You could hear it coming for miles, screaming, screeching, leaving clouds of dust a mile high. I was sure he would die on that thing."

"How old was he then?"

"About your age, sixteen, seventeen. He rode with his gun, too, an old Mossberg twelve-gauge. He shot snakes, crows, coyotes, jackrabbits, anything that moved or got in his way. Once I saw him shoot a pheasant with one arm *while* he was driving. No lie."

"Did he get into trouble?"

"Not with the law. The nearest sheriff was thirty miles away. Your grandpa almost killed him, though. He probably would have if your dad wasn't such a good worker. See, John, there's two kinds of work: light work and heavy work. Light work takes skill, planning, knowledge. Heavy work takes sweat, guts, muscle. Your dad was good at both."

"I'm not much good at either."

"You and me both. Your dad never tells you stories?"

"Not really. When did he change?"

"You've got to understand, John, he was never a bad man. Never. Just had his demons to chase, you know. We all do."

Peter brushed a fly from his eyes. He stared into the soft reaches of the sycamore. Something came to his mind and started him laughing.

"What's so funny?"

"There's a story you need to hear," he said. "But I'm not the one that told it to you, okay? You heard it from Uncle Robert. You got it?"

"Sure."

"One of your aunts, I won't say which one, used to be wild in high-school, wild and loose. She drank too much, drank like a fish. But she was stubborn and wouldn't listen to anyone. She made a lot of mistakes in a short time. One of these mistakes was getting pregnant by an older guy. Before she was showing, your father and I found out, and we went to have a talk with the guy.

"He worked at a lumberyard. When we got there, we found a whole crew of guys hanging around a basketball court on their lunchbreak. They were huge. I can still see their beards and their boots and their flannel. We were both scared to death, but your dad walked right onto the court and asked for the guy. A beefy, blond-haired kid left the game and came over to us. Your dad and him had a very short, very angry conversation. The game stopped and everyone came over.

"The guy couldn't back down. Not with his friends watching. He said the kid wasn't his. He said our sister got around. He told your dad to go to hell. Your dad just listened like he didn't believe a word the guy was saying. The guy got red in the face. He started talking faster and faster. Your dad just stood his ground. I swear he didn't blink for five minutes. The guy couldn't figure your dad out. The situation had him cornered and he didn't know what to do."

"So what happened?"

"He threw a punch."

"My dad?"

"No, John, the other guy. He punched your dad right in the face. Hard, too. Your dad dropped to one knee, but he jumped right back up. He got in the guy's face again and started yelling. 'Wrong, wrong,' he said. 'What you're doing is wrong.' The guy was cornered again. He put a forearm in your dad's chest to get him to back off. Didn't work, though. Your dad only got louder. Finally, the guy threw another punch."

"Damn. Did it land?"

"No, his friends grabbed him and held him back."

"His friends? Why did they do that?"

"Because they heard what your dad had been saying. They knew that he was right and their friend was wrong. You have to understand, John, it was a different world back then. People used to be brought up strict and hard. They used to know right from wrong."

"So my dad never fought back?"

"Not with his fists. He didn't need to. He had the truth on his side."

"So what happened to the other guy?"

Peter slapped a fly from his leg and grinned. "That other guy is your Uncle Robert."

Chiapas

Dave was dreaming. Not quite a nightmare but something close.
The kind of dream that gave you a headache, left you slow and
groggy for half the next day. He knew he was dreaming but he
was too tired to think, too weary to resist. He let the dream
carry him.

He was back in Asia. Kneedeep in the ricefield mud. The
red sun warmed and dried the mud. The red sun pulled sweat
from his skin, blinded him, stooped his shoulders, drove his
head toward the ground.

He couldn't keep up with the peasants. He wanted to help
them, but he couldn't keep up. They bent easily at the waist like
limber children. Their thin, bare legs slid through the mud as
if it were water. In an unbroken flurry of motion, their hands
pulled seeds from the clump, planted them in the mud, returned
to the clump. Dave lost most of his seed. He planted unevenly.
His great weight drove him deeper and deeper into the muck.
The line of farmers moved steadily across the field. Dave fell
further and further behind.

The soldiers. They stood atop the ring of hills surrounding
the field. With lazy arms across their rifles, they talked and
joked. They looked down on the peasants with contempt, mild
curiosity. Dave worked harder. He caught up with the peasants
as they reached the edge of the field. The peasants turned
around and started back.

Dave heard his wife's voice. He saw her atop the hills, her
hands full with small wooden crosses.

She offered crosses to a group of soldiers. The soldiers
turned their backs.

"Help us," Dave called to her.

She moved to another group of soldiers.

Dave was hungry, thirsty, tired down to his bones. His back ached. His neck burned and blistered under the sun.

The second group of soldiers ignored her.

She moved to a third. This group cursed and spat. They raised their rifles and fired into the sky.

The peasants worked harder, faster.

The soldiers laughed. They fired more rounds into the sky. A few fired into the field.

"Leave them alone," Dave said. "Help the peasants."

"No one is beyond saving," she said, moving to another group.

The peasants' hands moved with an animal quickness in and out of the mud. Their legs swished and sloshed in accelerating rhythm. Dave groaned.

More shots.

"Where is our tax?" the soldiers said. "Where is our portion?"

"Time," the peasants said. "Give us time."

When the peasants finished their planting, they huddled together in a corner of the field. They eyes moved fearfully from the soldiers to the field.

Morning turned to afternoon. The sun increased in strength as it moved across the sky. Little by little, the rice grew. A speckled green emerged within the field of brown.

The soldiers made their way down from the hilltops. The phone rang. Their rifles glimmered in the sun. The phone rang. The soldiers smiled as they came near.

"Dave?"

"Who's this?"

"It's Brent."

Dave rubbed his knuckles into his temple. Brent. Brent. Soldiers. He saw the sunlight on their rifles. He saw them come down from the hilltops.

"Brent," he said, blinking, forcing his eyes open. "What's going on? How are you?"

"Did I wake you up?"

"No. Yeah. Dreaming. What's going on?"

Dave sat up in his bed. He threw off his blankets, shook his head clear, glanced at the red lights of his clock. 2:21 AM.

"Brent? Are you there?"

After a few seconds of silence, Dave heard the strike of a match. He listened to Brent inhale, exhale, inhale, exhale.

"Chris is dead."

Dave tried to remember their conversation as he drove to the truckstop for some coffee. The conversation had been short, filled with long, empty silences. For every two or three questions Dave had asked, Brent had given a few flat words in answer. What happened? How did he die? Mexico. What was he doing? How did you find out? The paper. When is the service? Where will it be? Tomorrow. Here.

Dave broke eighty most of the way there. He pulled into his hometown, cruised the streets a while, then parked outside the football field at their old high-school. He rolled down his window and gazed across the field.

He waited, expecting a swell of emotion. Nothing came. He tried to think about Chris, but his head kept pounding, still stuck in the dream. Feeling guilty, he drove to Brent's place.

They sat down together on the front porch with a couple beers. Dave rubbed the sweat from his forehead across his sleeve. He took in the the cool air of the summer night. Brent leaned back in his chair. He wore nothing but an old pair of workshorts stained with spatters of paint.

They glanced at each other in between drinks. They tried to notice changes in the other man. Dave, always massive, had put on quite a few pounds, nothing his wide frame couldn't carry. The blond goatee helped his fleshy, babyskinned face, but he still didn't look his thirty years. Brent looked older. The two hairless crescents on his forehead had advanced deep into his scalp. After years of construction work, the sun had weathered and cracked his skin. The dense muscles of his calves and biceps pressed against his skin like veiny stone.

Dave held the cold bottle to his forehead and closed his eyes. "I'm sorry," he said.

Brent nodded slowly, rocking in his chair. "Thanks for coming."

Dave stared down the dark street and sipped his beer. He waited for Brent to talk.

Brent set his empty bottle on the ground. He leaned back in his chair, propped his feet up on the railing, and gazed over the streets into the hills. His eyes were tired, hard, vulnerable.

After three more beers Brent finally broke the quiet.

"Everything dies, that's a fact. Maybe everything that dies someday comes back."

Dave knew those words. He stirred the deep waters of his memory. An old song, he thought, Springsteen. Before he could remember the name, Brent got up from his chair.

"Come inside. I'll get you some blankets."

Brent believed in God. Not the stuffy Sunday-morning God he thought Dave believed in. Not the elusive, mythical Truth that Chris had spent his life searching for. Brent believed in a God revealed only in the darkest of places. If God was God, he had to be God everywhere, especially in the shit.

Brent loved stories about the last days of deathrow inmates, their conversions, their confessions. He loved the contrast between the dark prison world and the light that broke on the faces of the condemned, yet forgiven, men as they approached death.

Chris called this the Dostoyevsky in him. Brent remembered the summer morning that Chris showed up at his house with a giant smile and a giant stack of books. Brent read ten pages of *Crime and Punishment* before the summer grass called him away. Why read when you can live? Besides, why couldn't the writers just come out and tell you what they wanted to say?

The only book that Brent ever finished was *Moby Dick*. He loved that book. He read it under candles in his bedroom late at night. Melville lost his way from time to time, but Brent thought that any fool could see the greatness of the book.

He loved the sailing, the sharks and whales, the untamed and unfathomable seas. He loved Queequeg, the savage but friendly Indian harpooner. He loved the single-minded determination and force of will he saw in Ahab.

Brent still remembered the discussion of *Moby Dick* by his senior English class. The smart kids, the ones headed for college, debated the typological meaning of Ahab's name for almost an hour. When Brent couldn't take anymore, he threw his notebook against the wall. "You guys don't get it," he said. "The guy was just pissed off, really, really pissed off."

Brent understood Ahab's rage. He understood the outrageous and malicious strength Ahab saw in the whale.

Brent had bloomed early in life. On the grade-school playground, he had been a man among boys. Heavier. Faster. Stronger. He never experienced the gangliness and awkwardness that nearly every boy goes through.

In middle-school he dominated the football field. Terrorized it, his coach said. His official position was middle-linebacker, but he covered the entire field. He sacked quarterbacks, knocked runningbacks off their feet, knocked wide-receivers unconscious. He was fast enough to cover the deep ball and tough enough to crack heads with linemen.

Then sixteen came. On the field his play remained excellent. Off the field, however, he hid a quiet, sickening fear. The fear came every time he looked in the mirror. Other people noticed his manly whiskers and thick cords of muscle, but he saw what was really happening. The chemicals that had flown so freely in his youth had now run dry, completely and suddenly dry. He had stopped growing.

Helpless, he watched the other guys shoot up to six feet and beyond. He was stuck at five-eight. Five-eight for life. He trained and lifted weights harder than anyone on the team. This only made him stumpier and slower. By his senior year, he wasn't even a starter. Quarterbacks lobbed passes over his head. Wide-receivers and runningbacks used their long strides to blow by him. He knew exactly where to be on every play, but he couldn't finish when he got there.

Dave and Chris thought they understood what he was going through. They tried to encourage him. Brent listened to Chris with annoyance but also respect. Chris was even smaller than Brent. He knew nothing about football. He took his daily beatings on the practice field and never complained when he sat out entire games. Brent respected that. Chris had heart and guts.

But Brent didn't respect Dave. He saw Dave as a waste of size and ability. His giant frame could have easily packed on twenty more pounds of muscle if only he had the discipline. He practiced just hard enough to avoid the coaches' yelling, not hard enough to really improve himself. He made mental lapses in big games and, worst of all, he was unforgiveably soft on his opponents.

Despite all these weaknesses, Dave could still crush Brent coming off the line. On the practice field they collided a thousand times and Brent never got the better of these collisions. Brent came at Dave with all his power, arms up, shoulders square, legs grinding, only to be driven backward by Dave's sheer size, by the crudest and cruelest of all natural laws.

After the service they drove to Adams Park. They walked the joggers' trail in their white shirts and blue ties. Brent worked his way through a pack of cigarettes.

"I need to know what happened," Dave said. "What was he doing in Mexico?"

"I don't know," Brent said. "No one does."

"He was living with you before he left."

"Yeah."

"You guys must have talked."

"We talked. That doesn't mean I knew what was going on inside his head. You know how Chris was."

Brent stopped to light a fresh cigarette.

Dave waited. He knew Brent was still holding back. "I need to know," he said, his voice soft, cautious. "He was my friend, too."

Brent looked up at Dave. His dark eyes narrowed as he

blew a wide cloud of smoke through his nose. "You been gone a long time, Dave. A long fucking time."

"Maybe so, but I'm here now."

"Now ain't much good."

The two men continued down the trail. They passed in and out of shadows as they walked through the trees.

Dave wanted to defend himself. He wanted to jab back at Brent, say something sharp and humbling. He thought of several things to say, but he couldn't say them in the cool, restrained voice he wanted to use. In the end he swallowed his pride.

"I didn't see Chris much after college," he said. "We wrote a few letters over the years but never really hung out like we used to. Did he change?"

"Yeah, he changed," Brent said, most of the edge gone from his voice. "Chris was always changing."

"He said he worked a lot of odd jobs around town."

Brent nodded. "He hated the office world. It took the life right out of him."

"Did he work for you?"

"Off and on. Chris was a hard worker. Unfortunately, he was about as good at carpentry as he was at football."

Dave smiled. "I'm sure he tried hard."

"He did about every job there is," Brent said. "He worked in warehouses and restaurants, drove trucks, washed windows, mowed yards."

"I guess he just wanted to experience everything."

"Experience is fine. It doesn't pay the bills, though."

"You guys lived together most of the time."

Brent tossed his cigarette. "We had two or three apartments together. We started nice and basically worked our way down. It was like Chris hated money or something."

"I think he hated materialism."

"Materialism, money, whatever you want to call it. If I bust my ass every day, I want to come home to a nice place. But Chris had this whole philosophy of deprivation."

"You said he worked hard."

"He worked hard at shitty jobs. You can't make a living at those kind of jobs no matter how hard you work."

"He was smart enough to do anything he wanted. Why do you think he lived like that?"

"He hated rich people. He hated anyone with a nice car, a pool, or a big TV. I think he got this peasant ideal from all the books he read."

"He must have hated his parents then."

"He didn't hate them, but he basically cut all ties. You saw them at the funeral."

"His dad was pretty stoic, but I saw his mom cry."

"She wasn't crying for Chris. She was crying for her own broken dreams." Brent lit a fresh cigarette. "Chris couldn't live in their world. He felt most at home in low places, rehabs, shelters, halfway houses, places his parents wouldn't be caught dead in."

"What did he like about those kind of places?"

"I'm not really sure. He helped out, cooking, cleaning, whatever. Sometimes he went just to talk to people. He loved listening to street people's stories. Sick people, crazy people, criminals, he'd listen to them all day long. I don't think he realized that most of it was bullshit."

"That made him happy?"

"Chris was a lot of things, most of them great, but I wouldn't call him happy."

"How did he end up in Mexico?"

Brent paused before answering. "One day we were driving to Colton to see my brother. We stopped at this rest area along the freeway. There was a whole swarm of ambulances and statetroopers around this truck. I went straight to the bathroom, but Chris went over to see what was going on."

"What was it?"

"Mexicans. A truck full of dead and half-dead Mexicans trying to sneak into the country."

"They suffocated?"

"I guess. I didn't want to find out, but Chris was drawn to it. He kept trying to get closer and closer. The troopers pushed him back but by then it was too late, he'd already seen inside the truck. He started shaking and crying, walking around in circles. Eventually, I got him back to my truck. The rest of the way he just stared out the window.

"Right before we got to my brother's place he started talking again. He said he couldn't understand how a place could be that bad. He said he couldn't understand why anyone would go through something that terrible just to get out. A few days later he left."

Dave spent the next few hours alone trying to absorb everything Brent had told him. He didn't question the accuracy of Brent's descriptions, but he struggled to reconcile this new picture of Chris with the skinny kid he remembered from his childhood.

Something else troubled him. He still didn't know how Chris had died. He could tell that Brent knew, maybe not everything but more than he was saying. Dave thought Brent was trying to protect him.

"Would it be alright if I stayed around for a few more days?" Dave asked.

"That's cool with me," Brent said. "Don't you have to get back for school, though?"

"I still have a week or two until classes start."

"What about your teacher meetings and all that? You can't miss those."

"They're the same every year," Dave said, shrugging. "I'll make up some disease if I have to."

"Stay as long as you want."

Brent did know exactly how Chris had died, or, more accurately, how Chris had been killed.

On the day the vague, three-sentence obituary had appeared in the paper, Brent had gone straight to see Chris' father at his office. Brent didn't leave the office until he heard and saw everything.

While Dave drove home to pick up some more clothes,

Brent sat on his front porch. Deep in the shadows, alone for the first time in days, Brent cried.

He couldn't fight the pictures, anymore. He saw them every time he closed his eyes. He didn't know why he had been so determined, so driven, to see the photographs. Chris' father had told him everything he wanted to know. He had begged Brent not to look. Hearing wasn't good enough, though. Brent had to see for himself. Maybe the same force that had driven Chris to Mexico had driven Brent to look at the photos. Maybe it was pride, a willful arrogance disguised as strength and determination. Maybe it was simply a hunger and fascination for the darkness of this world.

Whatever the force, the images would remain—the neat hole at the back of Chris' skull, the front of Chris' skull splintered and unrecognizable, the legs chewed to tatters by wild dogs, the back covered with more burns and welts than original skin.

Brent wept for his friend. He gave up his unbearable and hopeless struggle to deny. He let the images sink, settle, linger. He let his mind fill in the terrible spaces, the carlighter as it clicked from the console, the panicked rise of Chris' breath, the flash and fire of the pistol, the dogs' excitement at first scent.

Brent lifted his bottle into the air. In a swift stroke he shattered it against the railing.

Dave pulled up an hour later. He found Brent on the porch still holding the broken bottleneck.

"Sit down," Brent said. "You need to hear the whole truth."

They headed to a remodel job the next morning. They worked slowly through the morning hours, thankful for the simple labor and sweat that took their minds off Chris. By early afternoon they were useless. They packed their tools and headed home.

They dozed off and on throughout the day. After a half-eaten dinner they returned to the porch.

"I should have told you sooner," Brent said.

"You were just trying to protect me," Dave said.

Brent stared at the beer in his hands. "No, I wasn't," he said. "I wish that was why but it's not."

"Why then?"

"I guess it was old stuff, things that shouldn't matter anymore."

"Like what?"

Brent glanced at Dave then looked to the street. "Forget it," he said.

"Maybe it's something I need to hear."

Brent tapped his beer against his knee. He wiped sweat from his neck then looked at Dave. "I guess I felt like you didn't deserve to know everything."

"Why not?"

"Come on, Dave. You started pulling away from us all the way back in high-school. After college you got neckdeep in all your church groups and church friends and quit hanging out with us. When you started seeing Jennifer, it was like you disappeared from the face of the earth."

Dave's head tilted and sagged as he listened. He cracked his neck then his knuckles. "Anything else?"

"I remember your wedding day," Brent said. "Me and Chris and Shawn were sitting at the back of the church. We kept looking around wondering who the hell all these people were. Even the groomsmen. We had no idea."

"I was going through a lot of changes back then."

"I know you were."

"I was trying to follow God."

"I believe you. I really do. I'm just saying you didn't need to bail on your friends to do that."

"I didn't bail on you guys."

Brent went to work the next day, but Dave stayed at home. Dave spent the day thinking, weighing the words of his friend, trying to make sense of the last ten years of his life.

He couldn't blame Jennifer for all his pain and problems anymore. Looking back, he had been just as overeager to get married as she had. At the time everything had seemed so right, so natural. He had been twenty-two, strong, healthy, happy to be a math teacher, in love with God, in love with a beautiful woman. All the pieces had come together so perfectly. He had no doubt that it was all part of a wonderful plan.

Brent was right. Dave had bailed on the guys he grew up with. Not entirely, but basically he had, at least for a few years. Dave felt a flush of shame when he thought about the groomsmen at his wedding. Brothers in Christ, brothers for life, he had thought during those early years of faith. Now those guys were gone. All the church crowd, too.

Jennifer's reputation had suffered from their marriage problems but not nearly as much as his. She had grown up in the church, deep in its safest circles. He had grown up on the outside, partying and playing sports with his friends. Jennifer knew the church language, the church culture. Unconsciously, she also knew the subtle maneuvers that could push another person down while still holding the charitable moral highground for oneself. His two or three beers a night somehow became a drinking problem that everyone knew about. His occasional swearing became an anger problem, another symptom of his distance from Christ.

All remaining hope for their marriage had been destroyed by one year in Asia. Jennifer's philosophy of missions had been to help the people by preaching and teaching. Dave had held this philosophy before they left, but after a few weeks in the field his thinking radically changed. The desperate physical needs of the people—basic sanitation, food, clean drinking water, immunizations, birth control—became his sole priority. Jennifer, and most of the other missionaries, regarded the physical needs of the people as important but their spiritual needs supreme. When Dave deviated from their programs and methods, he found himself an outcast. When he refused to ask forgiveness and re-enter the flock, he found himself on a plane bound for the States.

The divorce came soonafter.

Dazed and disillusioned, he survived the months after his

divorce like a sailor adrift at sea clinging to a few shipwrecked planks.

They woke up late the next day. They worked for a few unproductive hours under the August sun. When they realized they were doing more harm to the deck than good, they headed home.

On the porch, Brent ate a cold hamburger then lit up his last cigarette. Dave sipped a beer.

"You were right," Dave said. "I did bail on you guys."

"Forget it," Brent said. "I'm sure I wasn't a perfect friend, either."

"I never meant to, Brent. I just got caught up in myself, I guess."

Brent gave a dismissive shrug of his shoulders. "You know what I can't stop thinking about? Chris' last hours."

"I wouldn't think about that."

"Why not? In my mind, that's what everything comes down to."

"We should remember the good times with Chris: fishing on the river when we were kids, summer sleepovers in his basement, playing football in the park on fall days."

"That stuff's good," Brent said, "but we have to think about the way he died. Chris lived through that shit. The least we can do is try to imagine what it was like for him."

"He probably just wanted it to end."

"I don't think so."

"They tortured him," Dave said, his voice little more than a whisper. "Anyone being tortured just wants to die."

"No, I don't think so," Brent said, shaking his head with increased certainty. "Not Chris. If Chris still believed in what he was doing down there, he would have spit in their faces."

"Do you think he might have had regrets?"

"I don't know. I don't know what he saw down there. I don't know exactly what he was doing."

"He probably got involved with a political group, someone

radical like the Zapatistas. I thought Chris was a pacifist, though."

"When it came to fistfights he was. I'm not sure how he felt about war."

"I can't see Chris as a soldier."

"If he believed in their cause, he would have done anything for them."

Dave pictured Chris on horseback with masked face and a rifle in his hands. The image didn't fit. "Who do you think killed him?" he said.

"I don't think it was random and I know Chris wouldn't have gotten mixed up with drugs."

"Probably some sick paramilitary group."

Brent nodded. He tossed his cigarette butt into the grass. His small, dark eyes glowed as they looked to the southern hills.

They didn't work for the next three days.

Brent avoided Dave. He drove the hills for hours in his truck and said nothing when he returned.

Dave prayed. He read through his pile of old letters from Chris. He searched Chris' room and found a half-dozen notebooks filled with poems and journals. He read the notebooks again and again as he waited on the porch for Brent.

On the morning of the fourth day, Brent woke at dawn. He grabbed his bag, already packed, and left the house. He shut the front door softly, took in a breath of wet morning air, and lit a cigarette. Through the flame, he saw Dave standing at the edge of the porch.

"You weren't going to tell me?" Dave said.

"I knew what you'd say," Brent said.

"Yeah, what's that?"

"You'd tell me not to go. You'd tell me I was a fool." Brent took a long pull from his cigarette then pulled out his keys. "I love you, Dave, but I have to do this. Take care of yourself."

Dave followed Brent to his truck.

Brent threw his bag into the back of the truck. He saw

another bag and box already there. "What the hell's that?" he said.

"What's it look like?" Dave said. "I'm going with you."

"You're not coming."

"If I don't go with you, you're coming home in a body bag."

"No, Dave, I'm doing this my way."

"Your way is going to get you killed. That's if you even make it down there."

Brent's face twisted. He put his hand on the door of the truck. "I'm going alone."

"Your way isn't what Chris would want," Dave said. He pointed at the box in the back of the truck. "That box is full of Chris' writing. You're going to read everything in it. You're going to see that Chris wouldn't want revenge."

"Don't do this, Dave."

"I'm not going to lose another friend."

"Please don't do this."

"We're going down there to learn about Chris. Not just how he died, but how he lived his last days."

The cigarette dropped from Brent's hand. He leaned forward and beat his forehead against the glass. "Don't do this, Dave. I'm begging you."

Coma Dreams

Maybe the Rolling Stones can keep me awake. I've got two more hours in this car, two long hours on this dark country highway. I can already see Ryan lying still in his hospital bed. Take me away, Stones. Make me forget. I don't want to think about the hospital smells, the machines, Ryan's pale lips. Give me a few good songs and I might make it. I'll lose myself in the passing hills, the fields of hay and corn. I'll watch the breezes work through the wheat, watch the creeks carry the broken moonlight away.

The first time I saw Ryan was in third-grade. He wasn't much to look at then. Just a skinny kid with big ears and big hands. He had a sickly, shivering look to him like he had just emerged from a cold swimming pool. He never talked to anyone, teachers or kids. Most of the time he stared out the window as if hoping the playground grass would save him.

He disappeared for years, showed up for part of seventh-grade, then vanished again. When he reappeared my junior year, I didn't recognize him. He had been a six-foot stick in seventh-grade, but the guy that showed up in my geometry class stood six-three and solid. Only his big ears gave him away. He wore workboots, loose jeans, and a t-shirt stained with oil. His blond hair was shaved to fine stubble. Dogtags glittered and swayed over his chest.

He missed the first two days of class then came late on the third day without books, paper, or pencil. After watching the teacher lecture for five minutes, he got up to leave. The teacher met him at the door.

"Where do you think you're going?" the teacher said.

"My counselor screwed up," Ryan said. "I shouldn't be in here."

"You can talk to your counselor after class."

Ryan kept his eyes below the teacher's glare. He stared into the hallway looking ready to step past the smaller man.

"*After* class," the teacher repeated. "No one leaves during."

Ryan continued to stare into the hallway. The whole class watched him, wondering who he was and where he came from. The teacher stood his ground, suddenly looking like he hadn't slept in a week. Eventually Ryan sat down at a desk next to the door. He played with his dogtags and watched the hallway for the rest of class.

The next day I was surprised to see him come in and sit down next to me at the back of the class. He flipped the cover of his geometry book back and forth between his fingers.

"You're back," I said.

He shrugged.

"What did your counselor say?" I asked.

"Some bullshit about having to pass a class before moving on to the next one."

For a few weeks I tried to make small talk with him, but only received one-word answers and one-shouldered shrugs. I eventually gave up and stuck to my homework.

One day, uncharacteristically talkative, he turned to me while we waited for the bell to ring.

"Do you ride?" he asked.

"Yeah. Sometimes."

"Where do you go around here?"

"There's trails in the hills if you know where to look."

He nodded. "What kind of bike you got?"

"Mountain bike, Gary Fisher," I said, hoping to impress him. "How about you?"

He smiled. "Harley. Wear pants tomorrow. I'll take you for a ride."

I skipped my workout after school and met Ryan behind the gym. He showed up on an old model Harley, newly restored, and handed me a helmet.

"Nice bike," I said. "How'd you get a license?"

Ryan took out his wallet and flashed a license from another state. I nodded, impressed. Next to the license I saw a photograph of a much younger, thinner Ryan standing near a veterans' memorial in Washington, DC. A man stood next to him. The man was several inches shorter than Ryan but a foot wider around the waist. His grey and white beard covered all of his face except for hard, blue eyes. Long hair filled the hood resting over the back of his denim jacket.

"That's my dad," Ryan said. He checked his jacket pocket for cigarettes. I started to ask a question about his father but he revved the engine. "Hold on," he said.

We cruised through town then took backroads into the hills. The bike terrified me at first. I held Ryan's waist as the gravel of the road flashed by. I imagined what the gravel could do to my hands and knees if thrown from the bike. Gradually, I relaxed in the skill and confidence of Ryan's driving. I kept my eyes focused on his steady hands rather than the flashing road.

He drove to the city cemetery. We parked, kicked back on a bench, and stared over the headstones to the city below. Ryan lit a cigarette and offered me one.

"I don't smoke," I said.

"Good man."

"Didn't you want to hit some trails?"

"Not with this bike," he said. "Another time."

I scanned the headstones. "You know anybody here?"

"No, I just come here to get out of my house sometimes."

I stood up to avoid his smoke and stretch my legs. "You lived here before, didn't you? Third-grade, I think. Seventh-grade, too."

He nodded, blowing smoke through his nose.

"You remember me?" I asked.

"Yeah. You're the baseball guy."

I smiled, pleased at being remembered by him. "Where did you move?"

"Everywhere. California, Texas, Oklahoma, Mexico."

"Your dad in the military?"

"He was," Ryan said. He turned his eyes from the city and looked at me with pride. "My dad's a vet. Served three tours."

"What's he do now?"

"Not a lot. Works on bikes, rebuilds cars, chases women."

"What about your mom?"

"Don't know. Last I heard, the bitch was in a Texas rehab."

"Why do you call her a bitch?"

"You ever meet my mom?"

"No."

"Neither have I," he said. He ground his cigarette out on the bottom of his boot and stood up. "Let's get something to eat. You want to drive?"

Driving the Harley felt like trying to bullride a rhinoceros. I rarely ventured over second-gear as we cruised dusty backroads and country highways to a tiny Mexican restaurant.

Ryan stepped off the bike shaking his head. "Damn, John, that put me to sleep."

"Just being careful," I said. "Aren't you afraid of crashing on that thing?"

"Everyone dies," Ryan said. "At least I'd go out riding."

He spoke some broken sentences of Spanish to the waitress behind the counter. She nodded and slipped into the kitchen. In a few minutes she emerged with cokes and two plates of quesadillas. Ryan paid. We went outside and sat down at a wooden table surrounded by kneehigh wildgrass.

After the quesadillas disappeared, we sipped coke, spit ice cubes into the grass, slapped mosquitoes, and told stories. Ryan told me about roadtrips around the country with his father. I told him about baseball and my dream of playing pro ball.

The sun slipped under the last bank of clouds in the sky, lit up the hayfields in amber and orange, then vanished in the distant mountains. You could feel something. Summer was fighting, summer was dying. Another school year waited for us beyond this countryside. Part of me felt like anything was possible, part of me was scared. Whatever the year held, a storm of feeling told me that Ryan would be there with me through it all.

I met Ryan's father the day after our ride on the Harley.

A truck pulled up while Ryan and I were studying on his back porch. The truck door opened and closed. Heavy boots beat their way across the driveway. They stopped in the garage.

"Dad?"

The back door opened. The patio shook with his father's heavy steps.

"What's up, Dad? This is John."

I stood up to shake his hand but he ignored me. He moved toward Ryan.

The two stared at each other, Ryan looking up from his chair, his father glaring down. When his father spoke, the resonant and rough timber of his voice reminded me of Johnny Cash.

"Taking my bike without asking was a stupid move."

Ryan closed his book. He opened his mouth then closed it.

"You could have taken either bike of yours," his father said. "There was no need to take mine while I was gone."

Ryan's back stiffened. His thumbs dug into the cover of his book until the knuckles turned white.

"We'll talk more later," his father said. He turned to me, shook my hand, then went inside the house.

Ryan missed the next few days of school.

Early Saturday morning he cruised onto my driveway on a Yamaha with a bag of pistols and ammunition slung over his shoulder. I noticed some cuts around his mouth and a thin, purple scab down the middle of his lip.

I didn't think my dad would let me go, but after a long conversation with Ryan he gradually relaxed. Confident and knowledgeable, Ryan won him over. "Have fun," my dad said. "Be safe."

I hopped onto the back of the bike. Ryan watched as my dad went into the house.

"Your dad's a cop, isn't he?" he said.

"Yeah. I told you that, didn't I?"

"No. You can just tell."

I adjusted the small helmet as best I could. I waited for Ryan to start the engine, but his arms rested across the helmet in his lap. He stared at my parents as they waved from the living room window.

"What are they doing?"

"Just waving," I said.

"Why?"

"Come on, Ryan, let's go."

"Are they gonna videotape us?"

I gave my parents a quick wave. "Come on," I said. "Let's go."

Ryan shook his head and started the engine.

Deep in the hills we blasted milk jugs filled with stream water. I shot from close-range just to see water explode, but Ryan took his shooting seriously. He drilled himself for accuracy. He shot from different ranges and positions. He fired from behind trees like a sniper, drew from the hip like a gunslinger, dropped prone like a soldier under mortar-fire. We both delivered the last shot of the day execution-style.

With ringing ears we shared a cigarette under the trees.

"Why you smoking?" he asked.

I shrugged. "Whose guns are these?"

"Mine."

The twist of his head told me he was lying. "You must have a good job," I said.

"Me and my dad fix up cars," he said, "rebuild motors, stuff like that."

"That's cool. I wish I knew about cars."

"They're not that hard. You just have to take one apart and put it back together."

"Anything I take apart isn't going back together."

Tired of passing the cigarette, Ryan lit his own. "Hey, what kind of training do you do? I was thinking about starting my own program."

"In the offseason I run and lift weights every day but

Sunday. One workout is back, bis, and sprints. Another is chest, shoulders, tris, and long-distance. Once a week I do an all-legs day that ends with a hundred yards of lunges."

"That sounds tough. I need something with some contact, though."

"Me and some guys from the baseball team box in my basement."

"I was thinking about the martial arts. I love their discipline, their whole philosophy."

"Which one are you thinking of?"

"I don't know. Maybe tae-kwon-do or karate."

"We could still jog together and lift weights. Doesn't have to be everyday."

Ryan nodded like he heard me, but he was already dreaming.

He started with judo. He learned the basic flips and throws in a month then quit. "The art's too limited," he said. After judo he went to karate. He earned a few belts at the community center but again lost interest. Tae-kwon-do was the same, a few months, a few belts, and that was all. I told him he should enter some tournaments to test himself, but he shrugged me off.

In the spring, he came to every one of my games. Though he had never played baseball himself, he learned the game quickly. He met me at the dugout between innings to offer tips through the fence. Outside of the team practices, he became my personal trainer and motivator. He kept track of my running times, lifting max's, and baseball statistics in a notebook.

On many cold mornings the sound of his bike woke me up for our three-mile jog. I whined and complained, but he threw me clothes, fed me toast, and dragged me out the door. The jog always hurt like hell. Whenever I was ready to quit, I looked at the grimace on Ryan's face and borrowed from his strength.

His own progress in the martial arts completely stalled. I told him not to give up. Halfheartedly, he agreed to watch a jiu-jitsu tournament with me. He read a book during the early matches with the little kids and beginners. When the brown- and black-belts came out he dropped the book and leaned forward.

He talked to himself as he watched. He cheered for reversals, cringed for submissions, called out moves and counters. "It's fluid," he said. "It's beautiful."

Two Brazilians came out for the black-belt exhibition. Ryan couldn't breathe. With creativity and frightening speed, they battled each other in a chess-like struggle for position. After twenty tense and grueling minutes, one fighter left his arm unprotected for a fraction of a second. His opponent locked in an armbar and forced the tapout.

When the match was over, Ryan ran up to the winner. Ryan tried to talk to him, but his English was terrible. All he could say clearly was his name, Renzo. Ryan searched the crowd until he found an English-speaking fan that knew the name of Renzo's school. He enrolled the next day.

The summer before our senior year became the Jiu-Jitsu Summer. In exchange for English tutoring and floor-sweeping, Renzo opened up the world of jiu-jitsu to Ryan's ever-hungering eyes. They rolled on the mats for hours after official classes ended. Ryan learned all the variations of the mount and guard positions. He learned anklelocks, kneebars, armbars, chokeholds. He took his beatings like a man, always pressing his teacher for deeper knowledge.

Renzo made a fatal mistake when he gave Ryan a stack of videotapes from Brazilian ValeTudo tournaments. To me the videos looked like camcorded streetfights. To Ryan they were art. He watched the fights over and over. He paused the images so often that the tapes got fuzzy.

Renzo had no choice but to move from grappling to striking. He taught Ryan a Muay Thai style of kickboxing. Ryan learned the form of the punches, kicks, knees, and elbows then worked on his speed and power. He sparred with Renzo in long, brutal late-night sessions. Despite black eyes, bruised ribs, and swollen ears, Ryan became good enough to hold his own with Renzo on most nights.

In November of our senior year, Ryan entered his first, and last, tournament. A Japanese fighting school on a tour of the States scheduled an exhibition in our town. They promoted the exhibition as a goodwill display for the public and organized tournaments for each art form in the lower belts. After the tournaments, five superfights showcased the best of the Japanese masters against local fighters.

Manic with energy, Ryan called me two days before the tournament. "I'm fighting," he said. "Saturday night."

"Sweet," I said. "I've seen those tournament posters everywhere."

"Not the tournament," he said. "I'm in a superfight. Renzo broke his hand."

The crowd was mostly Latin, Brazilian I assumed, with scattered pockets of blacks, whites, and Asians. Quiet throughout the awards ceremony for tournament winners, the crowd came alive for the first superfight.

"Do you think he can win?" I asked Ryan's father.

He gave me a wry, condescending grin. "Ryan thinks he's unstoppable," he said. "If he taps out quick, he won't get hurt. If he tries to be a hero or does something crazy, he'll learn what pain is."

A Samoan fighter entered the ring. He looked ready to kill. Black-green tattoos covered his chest and back. His muscles looked harder than bone. A Japanese fighter entered the ring, bowed to his opponent, and removed his gi. Smaller, ill-defined in the upper body, he moved around the ring with slow, cautious steps.

"I can't believe they're letting these two fight," I said. "The Samoan's going to kill him."

"The Samoan's a punk. He won't last a minute."

"The guy's a monster."

"Tattoos and muscles don't mean anything at this level. Streetfighters like that guy get eaten up."

"So what wins fights at this level?"

"Technique."

"Technique can't eliminate the laws of physics."

"That's why the Japanese guy will take the fight to the ground. He's not stupid enough to trade punches."

"What do you think will happen on the ground?"

"Position is everything. The Japanese guy will improve his position until he finds a submission. He'll bend some bone or joint the way it isn't supposed to bend. He'll cut off air to the lungs or blood to the brain and the big guy will tap out."

The fight started and the the Samoan came out swinging. Before he knew what had happened, he found himself flat on his back. An anklelock ended the fight within a minute.

"Damn," I said. "You were right."

"At least there won't be strikes in Ryan's fight."

"What are you talking about?"

"Renzo made them change the rules. Ryan's fight is the only one without strikes."

"Why?"

"Because Renzo doesn't want his student to get his head split open with a high kick."

"That's going to crush Ryan's confidence. His own teacher doesn't believe in him."

"Ryan's fighting a pro, John. He'll be lucky if he isn't carried out of the ring."

A sick feeling settled in my gut as Ryan emerged from the locker room. His ears, already cauliflowering, stuck out against the smooth skin of his freshly shaved head. He was lean and cut, less fat than a marathon runner. He wore tight, black shorts and wrestling shoes. No robe. He seemed disoriented by the crowd. He blinked too often and kept touching his ears. The overdone intensity of his stare reminded me of a pro-wrestler.

Renzo lifted the ropes for Ryan with his good hand then entered the ring behind him. He grabbed Ryan by the back of the head, pulled him close, spoke into his ear, then kissed his cheek. He accompanied Ryan to the center of the ring for instructions from the referee.

The staredown was a study in opposites. Tan-skinned and baby-faced, Ryan leaned into his opponent with wild eyes. White-skinned and grey-haired, Shoji rocked gently on his heels and kept his eyes on the referee. Ryan looked down on the master from almost a foot. A single leg of Shoji looked thicker than Ryan's waist. The young man bounced on his feet, bobbing from side to side, bursting with energy. The old man looked ready for bed, irritated at being kept up so late.

"Get him, Ryan," I shouted, my hands shaking.

The bell rang.

Ryan came out fast, arms held high and extended, feet scampering. He shot in for a quick takedown, but Shoji sidestepped and threw a stiff-arm to Ryan's shoulder. Ryan paused a moment then resumed the chase. Shoji evaded. He used all of the ring, avoiding the corners.

When he was ready, the master settled into a wrestling clinch. Ryan's hands found the old man's biceps. Shoji let the hands grip. Shoji's weight dropped suddenly. Ryan sprawled his legs to block the takedown. No takedown came. The two fighters returned to the clinch. Shoji faked another takedown and again Ryan sprawled.

The real takedown came in a fraction of a second and left Ryan on his back struggling for position. His long legs tried to wrap around Shoji's waist but the old man bounded to the side. Shoji flattened his body on top of Ryan. He relaxed and used his weight to hold Ryan down. Ryan's eyes glistened with fear. He tried to spin and kick free, but every time he planted his heel, Shoji grabbed the ankle and stole Ryan's leverage. Ryan gave up before using too much energy. Both fighters rested.

Shoji improved his position through subtle shifts in weight and grip. He worked toward a submission on the left arm. Ryan couldn't see the move coming, but the crowd could. They stirred in their seats and started to cheer.

"Armbar," Ryan's father said. "Fight's over."

The armbar came swifter than the takedown. Shoji straddled Ryan's arm, locked his legs against Ryan's chest and shoulders, and rolled backward. His legs pinned Ryan to the mat while his arms worked to hyperextend Ryan's elbow.

Ryan yelled in pain.

The crowd jumped to its feet.

Shoji looked at the referee expecting him to stop the fight. The referee looked at Ryan expecting the tapout.

Ryan closed his eyes. He took a deep breath through his mouthpiece.

Shoji gritted his teeth and torqued the arm again.

Ryan didn't tap.

Slick with sweat, his captive arm twisted, jerked, and slid out of Shoji's hands. Ryan rolled away and hopped to his feet. Visibly frustrated, Shoji stood.

The crowd roared as the fighters squared off in the center of the ring.

Ryan was electrified. His eyes sharpened. The rhythm of his heart and lungs synchronized at a breakneck speed and pushed out hot sweat in a continuous stream. His posture changed as if his frame now carried a much greater weight and force.

Then Ryan did something incredible, something unbelievably stupid. He slapped Shoji. He lunged forward and struck Shoji across the cheek with an open palm. The resounding echo dissolved every other sound in the arena. The crowd booed. Shoji's eyes flickered through a moment of disbelief. He touched his cheek to confirm the disrespect done to him. Indignant voices shouted from his corner. Renzo said nothing and dropped his head.

The referee jumped between the fighters. He pushed Ryan back and gave him a stern warning. Ryan stared at the referee with confusion. His flood of adrenaline thinned as he sensed the rising contempt of the crowd.

The referee stepped back and the fight resumed.

Shoji rushed forward. The eyes above his red cheek burned with severe anger. Unafraid, Ryan faced the eyes and stepped to meet him.

The two clinched. Ryan tried to grab low, but Shoji blocked. He wrapped his arms around Ryan's waist then locked his hands against the tailbone. With all his strength, he lifted Ryan into the air, turned him sideways, and drove his head into the floor of the ring.

Ryan's body slumped. His eyes rolled back in his head. He lay on his back with one leg awkwardly caught beneath him.

His father jumped from his chair and ran to the ring.

Ryan's concussion was serious. On doctor's orders he had to be woken up every hour for two straight days. His father and I took turns. The first time I woke him, Ryan kicked me in the chest. After that I turned on his light instead of shaking him. From the living room, I heard him yell and swear every time he had to get up and turn off the light. One time I found him in the middle of the floor with no blankets, shaking and crying. Another time he came into the living room while I was asleep and grabbed me by the throat.

He missed every day of school in December. The day after Christmas I found him at the VA hospital.

He was hanging out with wheelchair vets in the snow-blown courtyard. The vets blew air into their cold hands. They watched birds fly between the ice-branched trees.

I could tell that he was coming down from a wild high. After staring at my feet for a full minute, he pulled back his hood and looked up at me with watery eyes that drifted in and out of focus. His hair had grown back since the fight. Thin blond whiskers covered his chin and the top of his lip. His cheeks were smooth and pale.

"Merry Christmas," I said.

"John," he said. He gave me a long, slow smile.

"Where the hell have you been, Ryan?"

"Here. Mostly."

"You don't look so good."

"I'm alright."

"Is your head any better?"

He shrugged. "I'm alright. You talk to my dad?"

"Yeah, he told me you were down here."

Ryan shivered. His head bobbed up and down. He looked away from me and stared into the trees.

I lit a cigarette in the cup of my hands and held it out to

him. He took a pull. "Thanks," he said. A few more pulls seemed to warm and waken him.

"I been learning, John. Been listening to these guys, learning their stories. I didn't know anything before. Not a fucking thing. Didn't know what life was."

"When you coming back to school?"

His lips twisted. "Don't know that I am."

"You have to come back. I miss ya, man. School's not the same without you."

Ryan gave me a weak smile. He handed the cigarette back, touched my shoulder, then turned away. A sadness came over his face as he gazed around the courtyard at the vets. "Spent my whole life feeling sorry for myself," he whispered into the wind.

That Christmas vacation my dad and I were at each other's throats. He wanted me to commit to a small, private college that offered me a full-ride scholarship. I wanted to go to the state university with a nationally ranked team. He saw the decision as a choice between stability and instability—one school guaranteed four years, the other just one. I saw my decision as a one-time shot at greatness.

"You can't play ball forever, John. That's a simple fact. What are you going to do when the game is over?"

"I don't know. I have years to figure that out."

"You don't have years. Next fall you start college classes. Every step you take from here puts you further down the path you're choosing."

"I understand."

"You have to think ahead. You have to prepare yourself. What if you blow out your knee or tear up your shoulder?"

"Don't put that into my head."

"I hope it doesn't happen but great players get hurt all the time, John. You're not invincible. You also need to realize that you're not going to be the best player in the league anymore."

"You don't think I can make it to the majors?"

"Forget major league. That's a million miles away."

"I thought I was supposed to think long-term."

"Think college," he said. "Think education. Think career."

"You don't get it, Dad."

"I guess I don't."

I got up to leave the room. My dad stopped me.

"John, you're my son and I love you. Whatever it takes, we'll get you through school."

I chose the state school. I told him before I went out with Ryan on New Year's Eve. He glanced up from balancing the checkbook, nodded vaguely in my direction, then continued working.

Ryan and I split a case of beer at his place before staggering a few blocks to a friend's party. We stayed till midnight then rode to another party in the back of a truck. Around two, a wrestler from another school tried to start a fight with Ryan. I grabbed Ryan before they could get into it.

Without a ride, we started the long, cold walk across town.

"You're coming back to school, aren't you?" I said.

"Might as well," Ryan said. "I'm bored as hell."

"You've got to graduate."

"Why? What does it matter?"

"We have to go to State together."

We climbed the fence to a schoolyard.

"So you made up your mind," Ryan said, hopping down on the other side.

"Yeah. I told my dad tonight."

"Bet he was happy."

"Hardly."

"You're taking a shot. That's what matters."

We crossed the schoolyard. Ryan stopped at the swings and took out a pack. "This calls for a smoke," he said. We leaned back in the swings, lit up, and blew smoke at the stars.

"I feel bad," I said, letting go of the cold metal chain.

"Why? If you go to the private school, you'll be miserable.

Their team's no good and you'd be surrounded by boring, rich kids."

"But they offered me four years. Everything paid for. That's a lot of money."

"Dreams and money don't mix. Your dad doesn't understand that. All he sees is the money. You have to be willing to give up everything for your dream."

"Can you imagine how it would feel to stand in the outfield of Fenway or Shea or Candlestick? Can you imagine the rush of taking one out of the park?"

"You can do it, John. You have the ability, the heart, the mind for the game."

We left the swings and trekked over the frozen grass of the schoolyard.

"What about you?" I asked.

"What about me?"

"Your dreams, man."

"Don't have any dreams. I'm just living one day to the next."

"You have to keep fighting, Ryan. You have to go back to jiu-jitsu."

"My fighting days are done."

"You just need a little time off."

He shook his head and spit.

"You can't quit," I said.

"I said I'm done."

"Why, because you lost one fight?"

"No, because my head's fucked up."

"You had one concussion. Athletes get them all the time. You have to be careful, but they're not the end of the world."

"You don't understand, John."

"I understand that you love fighting as much as I love baseball."

"Then why'd I lose?"

"You lost because you fought a guy with twenty years more experience."

Ryan turned on me. Even in the darkness I could see the

pain and anger that marked his face. "I can't train any harder than I trained for that fight. I can't sweat any more or bleed any more. Do you understand? I put everything I had into that fight and I got destroyed."

"Just don't quit. Give yourself a little time. You'll be a great fighter."

We hopped the fence out of the schoolyard. Ryan caught his hand on the way down. He held his hand under the streetlight to survey the cut.

"You alright?" I said.

He licked his finger then continued up the street.

"It's like with me and baseball," I said. "I still have more to learn about the game. I have to stay hungry and humble and keep learning."

"My head's fucked up, John. What don't you understand about that?"

"That's a copout, Ryan."

He stopped walking. "You talked about the rush of taking a ball out of the park," he said. "Well, I know how that feels. When I slipped that armbar I felt it, stronger than a mountain of heroin. I'm not talking about the crowd and the cheering. I'm talking about focus, union, perfect clarity of mind. I'm talking about every muscle and nerve burning wild but under total control. I'm talking about moving time with my breath— freezing time with breath in, melting time with breath out. I was so alive. So fucking alive. I'll never feel that way again."

"You will. Just don't give up."

We crossed a vacant lot. I felt hungry, tired, and irritatingly close to sober. I could see that Ryan didn't want to talk anymore, but something mean inside me felt like pressing him.

We entered the parking lot of a small shopping center. We walked along the sidewalk in front of the dark store windows.

"So what are you going to do?" I said.

"I don't know."

"Training was your life. If you quit fighting, there's not much left."

He gave me a glance of warning.

"Seriously, Ryan. You've already missed two months of school. Are you even going to try to graduate?"

He spit onto the sidewalk and lit a cigarette. He didn't offer me one or say another word.

Ryan missed the first week of school in January. I went to his house a dozen times, but no one answered the door. Eventually, I found his father walking alone in the trees outside the VA.

"How you doing, John?"

"I'm alright. You seen Ryan?"

"I think he's out riding."

I nodded and turned to go. Ryan's father grabbed my arm.

"Come inside," he said. "I'll get you a coffee."

We went inside the cafeteria, sat down with some steaming coffee, and made small talk. I could tell something was weighing on him. He needed to spill himself to someone but he didn't know how.

"You just hanging out?" I said.

"I came to see my doctor."

"How'd that go?"

He took a wad of papers from the inside of his jacket and threw them down on the table. I unrolled the wad, pressed the papers flat, and flipped through them. They were medical reports—blood tests, x-rays, biopsies.

"I don't know what these mean," I said.

"Neither do they."

"Can you get another opinion?"

"Won't make any difference."

"I'm sorry," I said. I set the papers back on the table.

He stared into his coffee. "During the war I got used to the idea of dying quick. Wasn't easy but I did. How can anyone accept dying slow?"

"No choice, I guess."

He watched a nurse walk by then set his coffee on the table. His shoulders drew inward and he shivered.

"If you can survive the war, you can survive anything," I said.

"The war's still killing me," he said.

He coughed spit into his napkin.

Ryan and his father left town a few days later without saying goodbye. Their house sold at a government auction in February and another vet moved in. I never saw Ryan's father again.

The school year crawled by. I buried myself in books and baseball to take my mind off Ryan's absence. Instead of plummeting like those of most seniors, my grades actually rose at the end of my senior year. Our baseball team won the district then lost in regionals. Despite a host of minor injuries, I led the league in hitting for most of the season.

Graduation was about as anticlimactic as I could have imagined. The ceremony seemed endless. Students took their obligatory photographs then scattered to small parties, most never to return.

After a grueling summer of roofing, I moved to the city and started college. The baseball manager arranged a nice apartment for me a block from campus. He set up my diet, class schedule, and workout routine. "There is no offseason," he said. Most of the other players I met were giant in physique and ego. I ate, lifted, studied, and partied with the guys, but they never became real friends to me.

Not like Hope.

The first time I saw her was in a cavernous, dusty lecture hall in the basement of the math building. She came in a few minutes late and had to sit in the middle of the aisle at the back of the class. The other late students made faces as they sat down on the concrete floor, but Hope didn't seem to mind. She pulled a pencil from her ear and a sketchpad from under her arm. She listened to the professor for a few minutes without taking notes. She lost interest and began to sketch.

Hope stood out among the other girls. To my eyes she seemed the only living, breathing creature in a sea of plastic dolls. She wore no makeup. Her clothes were simple and plain, probably secondhand. Her dark hair rested on the slope of her shoulders in knots and tangles. An arc of tiny studs lined the cartilage of her ear. A tattooed butterfly fluttered on the inside of her wrist.

For weeks I watched her across the classroom. I daydreamed and wondered who she was, where she came from, what she was drawing, what she was thinking about. Each class, as my courage and curiosity grew, I moved closer. When I finally sat down next to her and started a conversation, I was surprised by her voice. In all my daydreaming I had imagined a voice soft and sweet, whispery. But her real voice was bladed. The words came out rough and jagged, resonant and clear. Even the space between them held an edge.

When I asked what she was drawing, she shrugged, flipped the cover over her sketchpad, and slipped it under her arm.

"Just killing time," she said.

"Are you an artist?" I asked.

She gave me a tilted nod. I waited, expecting her to say more. She looked at the professor at the podium. Her eyes narrowed as she stared at him.

"I hate this class," she said. "Why should I have to study what he doesn't even care about?"

"He seems to know what he's talking about."

"That's not the same thing. He doesn't love what he's teaching."

"How many people really love math?"

Hope gave me a look of disappointment. She took out her sketchpad and opened to a blank page.

I knew I was losing her. The door was closing.

"What do you love?" I asked.

Her pencil halted on the page. She brushed a tangle of hair over her ear. "Music," she said.

"I love music, too."

She looked up from her sketchpad. "Yeah? What are you into?"

"Mostly early stuff. The Stones, Elvis, Buddy Holly."

Warmth and light filled Hope's face. "I love Buddy Holly," she said. "His music had this purity and simplicity, this amazing innocence. He was wild, too, but mostly innocent."

"Until the day the music died. What do you think about Ritchie Valens?"

"He was special, too. But when Buddy died, America lost part of its soul. That planecrash stole more from America than the bullets that killed the Kennedys."

"Imagine the music he could have written."

Her dark eyes dulled. "I don't know," she said. "What would he have done in the godless seventies? the ridiculous and greedy eighties?"

"He would have stayed true," I said. "Buddy was no sellout."

"Nothing gold can stay."

During our early days together, music was all we talked about. Burning ideas had long been trapped inside Hope. She was desperate to let them out. She had to test them, expose them. She had to share with another human being or risk losing part of herself. For some reason she chose me.

On bright-moon nights we drove into the country, parked among the wheat fields, listened to music, and talked for hours. Her opinions could be vicious. Elvis was a sad joke. Sinatra wasn't even an artist. The Beatles started as a boyband and never progressed much beyond that. Their lyrics were fluff, their songs advertising jingles.

She said that rock was born the day those German kids first heard the Rolling Stones and went completely insane. It died soonafter.

"What about Zeppelin, Rage Against the Machine, early Metallica?" I said. "There's been alot of great music."

"There's blood in the veins," she said, "but the beast is dead."

Hope's fatalism waned on good nights. She showed deep respect for jazz and classical musicians. She praised Joni Mitchell for her imagery and soul-searing honesty. Springsteen's album, *The Ghost of Tom Joad*, packed the substance of ten novels. Rage Against the Machine's *The Battle of Los Angeles* was a righteous battlecry for worldwide freedom.

"What's your music going to be like?" I asked.

"I don't know," she said. "I'm still young, still absorbing."

"Don't most musicians start young?"

"Some do, not all. I'm not ready yet."

"I want to hear some of your stuff."

"I'm not ready yet."

The chill of winter settled on the college town. Despite long hours of studying, my grades drifted toward the downside of the curve. Hope tutored me. She taught me how to skim the massive textbooks instead of reading every page. She showed me ways to scout professors and predict what would be on the exams. "You don't have to build brick by brick," she said after reading one of my papers. "It's alright to hop around a little. Try to make your writing fluid, organic."

Hope was right. I made honor roll by the end of fall semester.

I should have been happier than ever, but I wasn't. I couldn't shake a pain, a gnawing emptiness, that had been growing inside me for a long time.

"You miss him, don't you, John?"

"Yeah, I miss him. I don't even know where the hell he is."

"What if he doesn't come back? Maybe you just have to let go."

"You don't understand, Hope. We used to do everything together. Everything. He was closer than a brother."

Hope nodded like she understood, but I knew she didn't. She couldn't. Hope had never been that close to anyone in her life. She understood loneliness but not loss.

Baseball season started. The quality of college pitching completely overwhelmed me at first, both the speed and movement of the pitches. Shocked and frustrated, I spent more time on the bench than on the field. Everyone has to pay their dues, I told myself. I took my strikeouts in stride and learned from each one. I soaked up knowledge from the coaches and improved my patience at the plate. Still, my batting average languished under two hundred.

Hope became a sanctuary to me. My disappointment with

baseball faded during long nights at her apartment. In the glow of candles and the mist of incense, she played guitar for me and sang.

I remember the first night I heard her sing better than the first time we had sex. Within the misty candlelight, she ran her nails over the strings to get the feel. She closed her eyes and struck some chords, tuning. The chords eventually came together into a smooth, wandering movement. I tried to follow the movement but couldn't. When I thought the movement would rise, it stalled into isolated, bitter notes. When I thought the movement had lost its way, it returned faithful and resurgent.

Her voice entered the music sharp-edged and full. She breathed the words of a poem. I lay back, closed my eyes, and felt the force and sway of every word. Images passed—the stone fingers of a statue stirring, thawing; the dark green waters of the deep sea shivering; pale eyes lying. Without break or boundary, her guitar traveled through many songs, many poems. I gave up searching for story in the songs and simply let the music carry me. I listened, disembodied, dizzy with visions.

Hope played for me on countless nights.

The body of her music changed every time she played. Lyrics and lines recurred, but the body was constantly shifting and growing. She fleshed out parts of the body with detail, color, and intensity. Once grown, however, the parts threatened the unity of the whole. In frustration, her creative powers became destructive. She tore apart what she had carefully sown. She severed the organic. When she stopped playing, it was with a sense of defeat rather than completion. She turned away from me. She mumbled and made vague gestures if I talked to her. Without her voice the world returned in all its vulgarity.

For a while I thought that Hope was indifferent to my opinion of her music. Nothing could have been further from the truth. Deep in her heart, Hope believed that her music could awaken a sleeping world. She wanted her music to spread, to scorch, to pass over the land like waves of fire. I was the first to hear her music and also her first great disappointment. She wanted me to describe the high places, the states of mind that the music carried me to. I couldn't. Silence came to fill our nights together.

Ryan showed up at my door two weeks after baseball ended. I barely recognized him. He had the weathered skin and blistered lips of a homeless man. His hair was long, matted, soaked with dust and salt. He smelled of cigarettes, gasoline, coffee, come, and the dust of a dozen states.

I hugged him. "You're alive," I said.

He gave me a weary smile. The outsides of his eyes were more red than white. "Can I crash a while?" he said.

"Sure. You been riding?"

"Yeah. Since Tuesday."

"Straight?"

"Pretty much."

"Damn, you must be exhausted. Hey, Ryan, this is Hope."

She put out her hand but he didn't see it. He walked past her in the hallway like she wasn't there. In the bedroom he kicked off his boots, threw his keys and wallet inside his helmet, and collapsed on the floor. Hope and I watched him from the door.

"Don't sleep on the floor, bud," I said. "Hop in my bed."

He shook his head. He rolled over, took off his jacket, and packed it into a pillow.

"I'll be at class until late tonight," I said. "Help yourself to anything you can find in the kitchen."

He burrowed a little then sat up suddenly. "Is my bike safe on the street?" he said.

"I'll put it in the garage for you," I said, grabbing his keys.

Outside, I found the same Harley that I had driven in the countryside years ago. The bike had aged dramatically. Dents marred the fender. Dust stuck to the engine like fine cement.

"He hasn't slept in days," I said to Hope as I mounted the bike. "I don't think he even saw you."

She gave a self-protective shrug and glanced away. "He's not what I expected," she said.

"How's that?"

"From all your stories, I expected some kind of giant."

"Sorry to disappoint you."

"I'm not disappointed."

I turned the key. The engine started after three or four turns. It sounded much rougher than I remembered. I turned the engine off.

"What's wrong?" Hope asked.

"This was his father's bike," I said.

"So?"

"Nothing. You want to go for a ride?"

Hope looked at the motorcycle like Gandhi might have looked at a shotgun tossed into his lap. "No, thanks," she said. "I'll call you later, John."

Ryan was still sleeping when I came home that night. I woke him up at ten and asked if he was hungry. He sat up, glanced at me like I was a stranger, then looked around the room like he didn't know where he was.

"Grab a shower," I said. "I'll cook some dinner."

Even after a thirty-minute shower he still looked lost. He ate a plate of spaghetti without talking then leaned back on the couch. When the food settled into his stomach, he started to look half-alive.

"I like your place," he said. "Who's your roommate?"

"Don't have one."

"Damn, you have this whole place to yourself?"

"Yeah."

"Nothing but the best for jocks, huh?" He grabbed my bicep. "You're huge, man."

"Been training hard. I'm actually one of the smallest guys on the team."

"When's your next game? I gotta see you play."

"Season's over."

"I thought you played through April."

"Ryan, it's May."

He blinked a few times then grinned like he had been joking.

The phone rang. I let the machine pick it up. When Hope's voice came on, I muted the machine.

"Who's that?" Ryan asked.

"That's Hope. You met her when you first got here."

He gave me a puzzled look.

"You walked right by her in the hall, Ryan."

His face still looked blank. "She your girlfriend?"

"Kind of."

"Just a side-project, huh?"

"No, we're close," I said. "Hope's an awesome person."

"Can I smoke in here?"

"You're not supposed to," I said.

"What are they gonna do?" Ryan said. He pulled out his pack.

I walked over to the smoke detector and disconnected the battery.

Ryan lit his cigarette then rested his feet on top my table. After a few pulls from the cigarette, a look of pleasure came over his face. "Mexican girls were good to me," he said.

"You went to Mexico?"

"Yeah, me and my dad. We rode way the hell into the mountains. Lots of little towns, lots of little whores, lots of government guilt-money to spend."

We walked down to the garage and looked his bike over. Ryan scratched his key into the dirt embedded on the gas tank.

"Fucking filthy," he said. "I'll clean it tomorrow. Hey, how's your car running?"

"It's alright. No problems."

"We'll go driving tomorrow. You can show me around town."

"The next few days might be crazy. I've got finals coming up."

"That's fine. You want me to crash somewhere else for a while?"

"Where would you go?"

"I don't know. I could find a shelter or something."

I pictured Ryan standing in a dirty alley with a line of bums. "You're staying here," I said.

"It's no big deal. I've done it before."

"You're staying here."

"I don't want to mess up your school."

"You won't," I said, still fighting the image of my friend among the homeless. "You're staying here."

"Alright. Thanks, man."

"I have to get up at seven tomorrow, though."

"No problem. I'll get up with you."

I doubted that he would wake up before noon, but the next morning he came into my room at ten to seven with a plate of eggs.

Finals were brutal. I survived on a couple hours of sleep a night. Ryan helped out by cooking, cleaning, and keeping me awake. Night and day, he skimmed my textbooks and fired questions at me like a cross-examining lawyer. Sometimes I thought he was getting back at me for all the times I woke him up after his concussion. When my last final ended, we got five boxes of chocolate puffs, two gallons of milk, and three James Cagney movies. We fell asleep during the second movie and didn't wake up for a day.

The answering machine sounded like a bomb the next afternoon. Ryan crawled around blindly until he found the cord. He ripped the cord out of the wall in the middle of Hope's message. We tried to get back to sleep but couldn't.

"Let's go for a ride," I said.

I took Ryan to a quiet park in the hills. We kicked back on top of a picnic table, watched clouds drift by, and ate our convenience-store hot dogs. Ryan threw his hot dog into the garbage after two bites.

"I feel sick," he said.

"We'll start eating good now that finals are over."

He nodded painfully. "Sounds good. What's the plan for summer?"

"I was planning on going home. My dad said he'd pay me to paint the house. What are you thinking?"

"I was thinking we need to lay low. You've been studying too hard, I've been on the road too long. We should soak up the sun, watch old movies, sleep in till noon."

"I'm with you."

"Hey, could you park your car on the street if you had to?"

"Yeah, I guess."

"You don't need to paint any houses then. We'll get my tools out of storage and set up shop in your garage. We can work at night when it's cool. We'll start with a few bikes, move up to nicer cars. I'll teach you everything my dad taught me."

"How is your dad?"

"Gone," Ryan said. "He died in Mexico."

I grabbed his pack of cigarettes, lit one for each of us, and waited for him to talk.

"It's alright, John. He went out the way he wanted to."

"What happened?"

"Doctors couldn't help him. He was getting worse every day. One morning he woke up and asked if I wanted to go to Mexico with him. We took our time on backroads and old highways through Arizona and Texas. We slept at campgrounds and cheap hotels. We knew people along the way, but he didn't want to stop. He just wanted to be alone, you know, wanted to be free again. Riding made him happy, but he was fading fast. After crossing the line, we rode hard, straight into the mountains. We stopped in little towns to eat and fuck."

"You really slept with prostitutes?"

"I wasn't looking for a wife."

"Weren't you afraid of diseases?"

Ryan's cheek flinched. He shook his head to brush away the thought. "He was dying, man. The girls helped him forget."

"Did he die in his sleep?"

Ryan ground his cigarette out on the bottom of his boot then tossed it into the grass. "One day he woke up spitting blood. He could barely stand. We jumped on our bikes and rode through the morning, side by side, until we reached a canyon.

We pulled over and traded bikes. He took off his helmet and said to me, 'Ryan, you're my son and I love you. Remember the ride.' Then he coughed blood onto his boots, dropped his helmet to the ground, and tore off like a bolt of lightning. It was beautiful. He must have hit the guardrail at a hundred and twenty. His bike flipped and fell but he kept rising, soaring, flying straight toward the sun."

Ryan's eyes glistened as he savored the vision. The vision that inspired him made me feel nauseous and sad. Ryan saw his father only in the glorious ascent, but I saw the body at the bottom of the canyon, mangled and lifeless.

"He killed himself," I said, softly.

The wet sheen left Ryan's eyes. He looked down from the horizon and stared at the grass near his feet. "He didn't kill himself," he said. "He went out riding instead of flat on his back."

That summer we set up shop in my garage. Ryan bought used motorcycles, cars, and trucks through the classifieds. He fixed them up then made a few hundred dollars on the resale. He tried to teach me the mechanics, but I struggled. Most jobs took longer for him to explain to me than for him to do himself. By the end of the summer, I stuck to washing and waxing.

Hope borrowed my car to visit a sick grandmother in another city. Hope ended up staying there most of the summer. We talked by phone every week.

Ryan rarely talked about his father, but I sensed the weight of his pain. It sapped his strength and left him staring at the walls for hours. He loved working on cars, but even they could only take his mind away for a little while. I knew I had to do something.

On a rainy August afternoon I called him out from under a station wagon. He laid down his wrench, cracked the beer I offered, and sat down against the wall with me.

"How's she running?" I asked.

"She's not."

"You know what's wrong?"

"Yeah, I'm just not looking forward to fixing it."

I nodded and took a sip. "Hey, Ryan, I wanted to ask you something. I was thinking about not playing baseball this year."

"What are you talking about?"

"I barely played last season. Just fucking sat there on the bench."

"That's because you were a freshman, John. It was your first year. You were just learning, you know, adapting."

"I don't know, Ryan. If I wasn't playing baseball, I could spend more time studying. Besides, what's the point of all the practice and training if I just sit on the bench?"

"You must not be training hard enough."

I shrugged. I sipped my beer and watched Ryan. A light sparked in his eye.

"You've been slacking while I was gone," he said. "You need your old personal trainer back."

I smiled. "You think?"

That fall and winter our entire lifestyle turned monastic. No smoking. No drugs. No bad TV. No drinking, except Saturdays. Seven hours of sleep on weekdays, nine on weekends. We ran at least five days a week. We lifted weights six days a week, sometimes seven. Ryan adjusted my workout style after surveying muscle magazines. "Your workouts are too long," he said. "We need to keep them short and explosive." He was right. After a few weeks I burst through the old plateau and bench-pressed almost twice my weight.

Focus became the magical word to Ryan. Whenever I trained hard and gave all I had, he praised my focus. Whenever he thought I held back, he called me distracted. He blamed Hope for my distraction.

He rebuked me one morning while we stretched in the frozen grass inside the track.

"Do you know how many guys would kill to have your ability, John? You ever think about that? There's a million guys out there that love baseball just as much as you do, but God didn't give them half the ability he gave you."

I reached for my toes, felt the burn in my hamstrings. "I'm thankful," I said.

"How long have you known her, John? Six months? A year? You've wanted to play baseball since you could walk."

"Why can't I have both?"

Ryan gave me a hard stare. "You want everything, don't you?"

"I wish you could hear her sing, Ryan. If you could hear her music, you'd understand."

"I'm trying to understand, John. I really am."

Ryan got up from the cold ground. He rubbed his knees, grimaced, then gazed around the track.

"She has something special, Ryan. Something just as special as baseball is to me."

"Maybe. But that's her, John. You were born to play baseball."

I got to my feet. We stared at each other across frosty breaths.

"How far are we running today?" I said.

"We did four miles yesterday. We should do five today."

The first mile hurt. My bones felt dry, cracked. During the second mile, blood filled my bones and warmed my muscles. The pocket of air inside my chest condensed and I surged forward. Chemicals mixed and flowed, weight became strength, stride became synergy. I forgot about Hope and Ryan. I lost myself in the sweet pain and labor of the runner.

I held back on the third mile, afraid at the disappearance of limits I had long respected. I let go on the fourth. Ryan stopped running and watched from the bleachers. Two more miles flashed by, maybe three. I stopped counting. Organ by organ, I traveled through my body, prodding tissue, measuring flux in, flux out, pulse, response. Separating membranes dissolved, oxygen trails branched. My eyes dried against the cold track air. I could have run forever.

When I finally stopped, Ryan came out of the bleachers, his face radiant. He grabbed me by the shirt.

"That," he said, tapping my temple with two fingers, "has always been inside you. That will always *be* inside you. That's what I've been talking about. That's focus."

Dizzy, I stared into the blue and white sky. Every pocket of air above, below, and between the clouds flowed into my lungs. Ryan headbutted me and slapped my leg.

Though I defended Hope that day at the track, my feelings for her deteriorated in the winter weeks that followed. Ryan's words stuck in my head. I couldn't shake them. They haunted me every time I was alone with Hope. Under their unyielding counsel, I began to treat her with indifference, sometimes outright cruelty.

As the pressure of my classes and the intensity of my training increased, I pushed her further and further away. I expected her vicious side to emerge, but it never happened. I imagined an ugly blowout between us, but she never turned mean, unlike other girls I'd known. Her dark eyes absorbed each blow with a strange, quiet knowing. She turned her worst suffering into her best music. She let the pain sink deep then bled lyrics onto paper and played guitar all night. She found release in the music. Once gone, she waited patiently for the pain to return.

Hope joined a band that winter. To me, the guys in the band seemed undisciplined and strange. Hope loved them, though. She spent her nights practicing with them in the drummer's basement. Her guitar improved and she enjoyed the response to her lyrics from other musicians, something I couldn't give her.

I visited the basement once and heard them play. As near as I could tell, their music centered on atmosphere, a drifting, moody atmosphere. The rock songs began heavy and ended psychedelic. The slower songs, carried by a melancholy violin and Hope's haunting voice, digressed into arhythmic bass and drum solos.

On the last night before Christmas break, the band played at a local bar. Ryan and I got there early. We helped them unload their equipment then shared a pitcher with Hope.

"What are you guys playing tonight?" Ryan asked. "Anything I'd know?"

"Probably not," Hope said, lighting her fourth cigarette. "We don't do covers."

Ryan eyed her cigarette as he took a drink. She offered the pack to him, but he shook his head.

"We're training," he said.

"How about a celebration smoke?" I said.

"What are we celebrating?"

"I don't know. Surviving finals. Hope's first show."

I took two cigarettes from Hope's pack and held one out to Ryan. He looked away.

"No, thanks," he said.

"Come on, Ryan. Let's celebrate."

He shook his head. "I'm training," he said. "So are you."

"Fuck it," I said. I put the cigarettes back in the pack.

Hope didn't notice. She stared at the incoming crowd. Her fingers twitched on the table as she struck rapid, imaginary chords. Her lips moved in soft mumbling.

Ryan watched her. "You're scared," he said.

She didn't hear him.

"You're scared," he repeated.

"A little," she said.

"If you get scared, you're finished," he said. "You're done."

"I didn't expect this many people."

Ryan looked around the bar. "This is nothing. Try fighting in front of a thousand people."

Hope ground her cigarette out. She turned from the crowd to stare at Ryan. Ryan's hand slid over the drops of water on the outside of his glass.

"You'll be fine," he said. "John says you're a great singer."

Hope returned to the stage.

After almost an hour of setup and tuning, the lights finally went down.

Blue light filled the stage. Dust and smoke swirled in columns. Seated on a stool centerstage, Hope lifted the neck of her guitar and struck the opening chords. The rest of the band followed her lead.

Within a minute, the band had lost the crowd. A few sober members of the audience settled into chairs and listened, but most turned their backs. Unable to find a singalong chorus or heavy beat they could dance to, the crowd returned to their beer games and flirting.

"They're dying up there," I said.

Ryan's eyes didn't move from the stage. The hardness left his face as he listened to the music. "I was wrong about her," he said.

After the first song, Hope gazed across the crowd. A bitter smile crossed her face. She turned her stool sideways, exchanged glances with the guitarist, then started the second song.

I spent the rest of the night wrapped in a halo of beer. Ryan left the bar in the middle of the fourth song. Some baseball players joined me for a few pitchers then hooked up with random girls. The band struggled through a dozen songs then quit. They left the stage without applause.

I waited for Hope. She clung to the wall as she made her way toward me.

"You were good," I said.

She pulled her coat around her shoulders and glanced around the room like she was in danger.

"Get me out of here, John."

I took her hand and led her through the crowd.

Outside, we found the streets blanketed with snow. Hope leaned against a brick wall and lit a cigarette. Her eyes narrowed as she watched the crowd spill onto the street.

"Are you okay?" I said.

Hope shivered. She glanced at me, but didn't answer.

"I'll take you home," I said, kicking snow from my feet. "Let me find Ryan."

She nodded without taking her eyes from the people in the street. When I turned to go, she grabbed my arm. "I don't want to be alone tonight, John."

I wandered up and down the street several times before I spotted Ryan beneath a streetlight.

He was arguing with a football player, a cocky wide-receiver I knew from the gym. Both of them were stumbling drunk, both close to throwing a punch. Just walk away, Ryan, I thought. The guy's a punk. Just walk away.

Ryan didn't walk away. A few seconds later Ryan turned his head to spit and the wide-receiver's arm flicked forward. The punch caught Ryan below the eye. He slipped on the snowy concrete and went down.

Before I could get there, Ryan jumped up. He grabbed the wide-receiver's leg and took him to the ground. They rolled, wrestled, and slugged their way over the snow and slush. A crowd gathered. I followed the fighters down the street with the rest of the mob. I waited for an opening in the flurry of fists and knees to grab Ryan.

At the sound of sirens, the crowd disintegrated. I wrapped my arms around Ryan's waist and lifted him up. "Let's get out of here," I said.

Ryan found his balance, but jumped right back on top of the wide-receiver. A flood of light surrounded us.

For twenty minutes the police made us stand in the cold. They took our IDs, shined lights in our eyes, and asked a dozen questions. They examined the wet, red, and dirty faces of the fighters then went inside the police car and took out their clipboards.

"Fuck, Ryan, they're going to arrest us."

"No, they're not," he said. He stared across the hood of the police car at the wide-receiver.

While we waited in the cold, another police car flashed its lights a block away as it pulled over a truck.

The officer near us dropped his clipboard and rolled down his window. He handed back our IDs. "Go home and get some sleep," he said. "If I see any of you again tonight, you're going to jail."

The car pulled away.

"Thanks, officer," I said. "Thank you very much."

The space between the wide-receiver and Ryan stood empty. The wide-receiver threw a quick glance at Ryan then headed up the street.

Ryan followed him. "Where ya going, bitch?" he said.

The wide-receiver looked over his shoulder. "Let it go, man," he said. "I don't want to fight no more."

"Come on," Ryan said. "Finish what you started."

Ryan's feet quickened. I stepped in front of him. Our foreheads collided. He brushed me aside with a hard forearm to the chest.

I watched Ryan and the wide-receiver trade right hands. They both staggered backward. Eager to avoid another punch, the wide-receiver lowered his head, stumbled forward, and tied Ryan up. Ryan allowed the arms to grab around his waist, but slipped his wrist underneath the wide-receiver's chin. He sunk a guillotine-chokehold deep into the wide-receiver's throat.

When the police spotlight returned, Ryan stood over the wide-receiver who lay in the snow like he was sleeping.

Hope dropped out of school in January. She moved in with the guitarist from her band and got a job at a coffeeshop. Every time I saw her around town, she had a cigarette in her hand and the smell of weed on her jacket.

I didn't visit Ryan for a month.

On a rainy Saturday in February, I drove to the county jail. Inside, I waited at a table sticky with soda and sweat. I glanced around at the other visitors and tried not to imagine the lives behind their tired faces.

A line of orange-suited jailbirds entered the visiting room. Ryan, last in line, saw me and sat down at my table. The bones of his face seemed sharper than I remembered. The sickly color of his skin reminded me of the little boy in my third-grade class.

"Where the fuck have you been?" he said.

"Busy," I said. "Classes are killing me."

"Bullshit," he said. "You just started the semester. And

what about break? You couldn't leave the family fireside for one day?"

I endured his cold stare. There wasn't much I could say. He shook his head, squinted slightly, and glanced around the room at the other visitors.

"What'd they end up charging you with?" I asked.

"Everything," he said, turning his cold eyes back to me. "Cops don't like it when you fight back."

"You remember everything that happened that night?"

"Yeah."

"You remember hitting me?"

"I didn't hit you."

"When I tried to hold you back, you walked right into me like I wasn't there. We collided heads. You hit me with your forearm."

"My forearm? I hit you with my forearm?"

"Yeah, Ryan. You hit me with your forearm. You knocked me out of the way."

Ryan's eyes squinted again. The skin beneath his cheekbones stretched. "Why did you get in the way?"

"To stop you from getting arrested, man. To stop you from ending up in a place like this."

He motioned his head toward the cells with a dry smile. "You think this is the end of the line, John? the gutter?"

I lifted my leg from the sticky seat and leaned forward. "Look, Ryan, I'm sorry I haven't visited you till now. I guess I was pissed at you for disrespecting me that night."

Ryan leaned back. Weighing my words, he pressed the knuckles of his left hand between his thumb and forefinger, then rubbed a patch of whiskers under his lip.

"You got any change?" he asked.

I gave him a couple bucks. He went over to a vending machine and bought a candy bar and a coke. He came back and held out the coke for me.

"Go ahead," I said.

He cracked open the coke. He swallowed half the candy bar in one bite. "I'm so fucking hungry," he said.

"How's the food in here?"

"You don't want to know."

"Maybe we could find a good lawyer and get you out early."

"No, it's alright. I only have a few more weeks."

"You don't want to spend them in here."

He shook his head. "I hate lawyers."

"I've got a little money."

"I'm alright, John. It's not that bad in here."

He choked down the second half of his candy bar. He swallowed some coke then rolled up his sleeve. A fresh tattoo covered his right shoulder.

"Check it out," he said.

"Who the hell is that?"

"It's Che, man. Che Guevara."

I touched the ragged, green-black ink.

"It's sweet, huh? This Mexican did it for me. He said his cousin actually met Che after the revolution."

"You sure you want this guy's face on your arm for the rest of your life?"

He shrugged. "Why not? Che was a man among boys."

"Didn't he hate America?"

"He hated American imperialism. He hated the poverty he saw in Latin America."

I took a pack of cigarettes from my shirt pocket and slid them across the table. "I almost forgot."

Ryan tore them open. I threw him a book of matches.

"You been sticking to the program?" he asked as he lit up.

"Yeah. Baseball's starting soon."

He closed his eyes and held the first breath of smoke deep in his lungs. He gave a smile of pleasure when he finally exhaled. "You've been slacking, haven't you?"

"No, I've been lifting and running."

"How many times a week?"

"Four, sometimes five."

"That's not enough."

"It's kind of hard when my training partner is in jail."

Ryan's smile widened. He tapped ash into the coke can then leaned back. His shoulders loosened as the nicotine reached his brain. "Where's our revolution, John?"

We talked until an officer entered the room and announced the end of visitation.

Ryan took a last pull. He dropped the cigarette into the can and stood up.

We shook hands across the table. He held on and pulled me toward him. "I never meant to disrespect you, John," he said in a low voice. "You know that, right?"

"Forget it, Ryan."

"I just lost my head for a second, you know. Won't happen again."

"Forget it. It's done."

After a long, last look, Ryan let go of my hand. He turned and fell in line with the other prisoners.

Ryan got out of jail just in time to see my first baseball game. I started the game in right-field, but went 0 for 3 at the plate. After two more hitless games, the manager moved me to backup. My hitting slump continued into the heart of the season. The conditioning coach altered my training routine three or four times then gave up. I moved from backup to pinch-hitter to pinch-runner to a waste of a uniform. By midseason my scholarship was in danger.

"I don't understand it," Ryan said. "You're in the best shape of your life."

"There's more to hitting than conditioning," I said. "I can't get my timing right."

"What are you going to do?"

"I don't know. At least my fielding is good."

Ryan nodded, thinking. "You should move to the infield. Maybe try third-base."

"I haven't played infield since high-school."

"You've got the arm. A third-baseman that can take the ball out is rare."

"So is a third-baseman batting one-twenty."

"This slump can't last forever, John. Stay in the fight until the fight goes your way."

"I'm not giving up."

"Talk to your coach. Convince him to give you a chance at third-base."

I got my chance against the private school that had offered me a full ride two years earlier. The first groundball hit my way took a bad bounce, clipped the bottom of my glove, and cracked my shin. With a few hundred fans watching, I hopped around on one leg shaking the pain out. Both dugouts laughed.

Ryan met me at the fence between innings. "No one's going to remember that if you take the first pitch out of the park."

I watched the first pitch go by, but cracked the second pitch deep into left-field. The outfielder ran out of room and the ball sailed over the fence.

Two more singles and the slump was over. I started the next two games and went 3 for 8. A torn shoulder cost me the starting position, but I saw plenty of action the rest of the season. Though I wasn't a star and never would be again, I proved that I could play ball.

At the end of the season, the manager called me into his office. He congratulated me on my comeback then told me he had accepted a job at another school. I asked him about my scholarship. "Keep your grades up," he said. "I'll put in a good word for you with the new manager."

My grades came in the mail the same day as a letter from the new manager. I found Ryan underneath a pickup in the garage and held up both letters.

"I'll open my grades," I said. "You open the baseball letter."

He wiped his hands on his shirt. "Which one first?"

I took a deep breath then tore open the grades. My eyes jumped straight to the five letters in the far right column. Four B's and an A.

Ecstatic, I shadowboxed around the garage. Ryan lifted me into the air in a bearhug.

"You deserve it, John," he said.

"Your turn."

He set me down then used a screwdriver to open the letter. I watched his eyes move from line to line down the page. He stopped halfway, dropped the letter to the floor, walked over to the pickup, and drove his screwdriver through the windshield.

I avoided my parents' phone calls for a week while Ryan and I went on the drinking binge of a lifetime. We drank case after case of cheap beer and watched movies like *Scarface* and *Apocalypse Now*. The beer didn't help but the movies did. Ryan said anything and everything to make me feel better.

"The new coach is a dumbass," he said. "I heard he got busted for recruiting violations at his last school."

"Doesn't matter."

"It does matter. You're better than half those guys he brought with him."

"I didn't hit, Ryan. That's the bottom line."

"You had a few hitting slumps, but your fielding was phenomenal."

"I don't know what I'm going to do next year."

"Your parents will help you out. They want you to stay in school."

"I should have taken the other scholarship. My dad was right."

"You took a shot, John. How many people have the guts to do what you did?"

I shook my head. "What could I have done differently? Could I have trained harder, practiced longer, learned more?"

"You did everything."

"And it wasn't enough. Fucked-up knees, torn-out shoulder, ten-thousand hours of practice. Never enough. I was born to play baseball. What do I got now?"

Ryan worked his hands. He cracked his fingers like he wanted to pull them out of their sockets.

In the middle of our binge, on a hot summer morning, Hope showed up at my door.

"I came to say goodbye," she said.

I squinted from the bright sunlight. "How ya been, Hope?"

"I just came to say goodbye. I'm going to Europe."

"What are you talking about? Come inside."

"The car's running," she said.

Barefoot, shirtless, I followed her to the street. Bags and guitarcases filled the back of her car. The drummer from her band glanced at me from the passenger seat then looked away.

"What are you doing?" I said.

"Leaving," she said. Her dark eyes bore the bright sun without blinking. "I'm going to Europe."

"Why?"

She shrugged. "Got the urge for going."

"Is the whole band going with you?"

"Yeah. David knows some people in England. Eric knows some in Norway."

"You got a record deal."

"Maybe. It's a longshot."

"So you're just going to leave?"

She gave me a bitter smile. "Why not? What's keeping me here?"

I felt the accusation in her words. "You don't know what's been going on with me, Hope."

"You're right. How would I?"

I should have told her about my lost scholarship. I should have told her I was sorry for blowing her off for months. Instead, groggy, hungover, stupid, I just stared at the guitarcase in the back of the car.

"Take care, John."

Ryan hit the road that summer. He said he needed to clear his head and promised to be back by fall.

I returned to my parents' place. During the days I scraped, primed, and painted their house. During the nights I sat alone and stared at the walls. My parents watched me sink until they couldn't take anymore. Separately, they cornered me for heart-to-heart talks. My mother blamed Hope for my unhappiness. My father blamed baseball and Ryan.

"I don't think things are as bad as they seem," my father said. "Your grades are good. That's most important. That's your future."

"What about baseball?"

"Baseball's a beautiful game, John, but it's not life. You need to build a life without baseball. I don't mean a life entirely without baseball, I mean a life without baseball at the center. Maybe you could have fun just playing intramurals or coaching Little League."

The idea of going from a stadium to a Little League park made me sick and sad. "I could still walk on the team in the spring. Maybe get my scholarship back by my senior year."

My father exhaled with frustration. "You're wrecking your life and your body, John. It's not worth it."

"What do you think I should do?"

"Your mom and I talked. We can afford to keep you in school for a couple more years. It'll hurt but we can do it. We need you to walk the straight and narrow, though."

"What does that mean?"

My father leaned forward. "You have to protect yourself, John. You have to be smart. I knew guys like Ryan growing up. If he doesn't join the military, that boy is penitentiary bound. I don't want him taking you down with him."

Ryan didn't join the military. He said he couldn't forgive them for what they did to his father. He came back in the middle of September ready to engineer my comeback. When I told him I wasn't playing baseball, he looked at me with disgust.

"So that's that?" he said.

"For now."

Ryan didn't talk to me for a week. He slept in every morning, tinkered with his bike in the afternoon, then watched TV all night. We bumped shoulders in the hallway of our cramped new apartment without saying a word.

One day he picked me up on campus and took me for a ride. We cruised the hills for a while then stopped in the park. We sat down at the same bench that he had first told me about the death of his father. He laid his pack of cigarettes on the table, but neither of us reached to take one.

"We're living in fallout," he said. "All the shit that's happened, all the death and heartache and busted dreams, it's caught up with us."

"So what do we do?"

"I don't know. Just wait it out, I guess."

"Weather the storm."

He nodded and played with his lighter.

I stared at the clouds. I tried to lose myself in their lazy drift, but the death and heartache and busted dreams pulled me back.

"Check out these hoodlums," Ryan said.

A pack of boys rode by on dirtbikes. They jammed their brakes to see who could leave the longest tire streak. Ryan smiled.

"We can still work out," he said, "even if you're not playing baseball."

"Yeah, we should start up again."

"Without baseball we'll have more time on our hands. We can live in the weight room."

"Sounds good. Are you going to keep working on cars?"

"No, I suppose I'll have to get a real job soon. Gotta pay my debt to society, I guess."

"What'll you do?"

"I have no idea."

Ryan found several jobs, all of which he hated. He boxed groceries, pumped gas, hauled wood, and stripped roofs. Though he came home exhausted most days, he worked out with me three or four times a week. Our workouts became simple and routine. They lacked the old explosion and excitement. We used to believe that our bodies had no limits, that with enough heart anything was possible, that guts and willpower ruled the world. Now we just trained to avoid getting fat.

Something dark grew inside Ryan as he passed from job to job, something twisted and bitter. I think it started with the way college girls looked at him when he pumped their gas. It deepened each time a fraternity guy gave him attitude at the grocery store, each time a rich professor bitched about a dropped shingle in his flowers or some dust on his Mercedes. I imagine that Ryan daydreamed during the long, creeping hours at work to make the time bearable. He must have dreamed of his bike and his father and of the endless road stretched out before them. But I think his dreams only added to his rage.

Even after years of scouring my memory, some of the details of Ryan's last night remain a mystery to me. Like how did I get to the county hospital? I know I didn't walk the two miles from the bar to the hospital. I know I didn't drive because Ryan had the keys to my car. I'm sure I didn't ride in the ambulance, either, because I remember the paramedic slamming the door in my face. The police didn't take me, and I sure as hell didn't get a ride with one of the guys Ryan fought.

Even during the trial some parts of the story never quite made sense. Several witnesses claimed that the fight started when Ryan grabbed John McIntyre (I learned his name at the trial) by the shirt and headbutted him. But a girl, who claimed to be totally sober that night, testified that the fight started when Ryan slapped McIntyre. So which started the fight, a headbutt or a slap? I can't imagine that Ryan would headbutt a guy and *then* slap him. That would be like stabbing a guy and then messing up his hair. So either the only sober witness at the scene was mistaken and Ryan never slapped McIntyre, or the majority of the witnesses missed the real cause of the fight.

None of that mattered, though. The bouncer was the one on trial, and the legal question at hand was whether he had intended to harm Ryan or not. The chorus of witnesses testified that he had not. Their impressions varied slightly, but every one of them agreed that the bouncer had merely acted to separate the fighters. They testified that the bouncer had slipped on the beer-stained floor as he grabbed Ryan from behind. They said that the bouncer had only been trying to pull Ryan out of the fight. They said that Ryan striking his head against the corner of the steel chair had been completely accidental.

I remember that night differently. I remember the angry look on the bouncer's face after he swallowed one of Ryan's elbows, the white burning of his face as he wrapped his arms around Ryan's waist. I remember the vicious twist of their bodies, the sickening crunch of Ryan's skull shattering inward. Did the bouncer intend to harm Ryan? Did he really slip as he pulled Ryan from the fight? Did he see the chair sitting three feet to his left? Only God knows.

Sometimes I'm thankful for the haze of alcohol that dulls my memory of that night. Full reality would probably crush me. Of course if Ryan and I hadn't been drunk, the fight might never have happened at all. When I saw John McIntyre and his two friends on the witness stand, I wanted to hate them but I couldn't. They were guys, just like me and Ryan. Maybe McIntyre bumped shoulders with Ryan, or stared a little too long, or wore the wrong kind of shirt that night. Did he deserve to have his nose broken? No more than Ryan deserved what happened to him.

From the medical report I learned that Ryan had regained consciousness for several minutes in the ambulance. I tracked down one of the paramedics at the hospital.

"Did he say anything?" I asked.

"Yeah, he was talking."

"What did he say?"

"I don't remember."

"Try. Please try."

"It was mostly incoherent."

"Mostly? So some of what he said made sense."

"Not really. I don't remember."

Incoherent or not, I'd give anything to hear Ryan's final words.

They performed three surgeries in two days, but he never regained consciousness. My parents sat next to me in the waiting room when the doctor came out of the last surgery.

"He's entered a coma," the doctor said.

"Ryan's dead," I said.

The doctor's mouth opened. He touched his glasses. "No, he's not. He's entered a coma."

My mother put her arm across my shoulders. My father asked the doctor a question. I watched the doctor speak, but couldn't hear a word.

On graduation day I stared at the diploma in my hands. How had I gotten here? I remembered shaving that morning but I couldn't tell you the names of the classes I had taken over the last two years.

The drifting continued into the long, slow years after college. I moved to a city on the ocean, three hours from my parents, two hours from the bed where Ryan lies. I found a quiet little apartment, a German shepherd, and a good job. I take the bus to work every morning, come home about six, walk the dog, watch TV, drink two beers, and go to bed by ten. On Friday nights I rent a movie and drink three beers.

I hit the road almost every Saturday afternoon. In the winter I take the freeway in case of snow. The rest of the year I take the highways and the windy backroads. I leave home just before dark so that I can catch the sunset on the hills and the long, purple shadows of the wheat. After I check into the hotel, I lay on the dusty bed for a while and watch the ceiling fan spin. When I feel ready, I walk to the convalescent center.

I take one last breath of fresh air before stepping through the double doors. I hurry up the hall but can't outrun the smell. The mixed odors of human waste, rot, and neglect settle into my throat and burn my nose. None of the nurses make eye contact with me. They know that I'm going to complain about something as soon as I see Ryan's room. Why shouldn't I?

Sometimes his room smells worse than the hallways. Sometimes the stereo that I bought him is stuck on the Spanish station or country music. I've found the window cracked in the middle of winter and the fan broken in the heat of summer.

I close the door behind me and take my first look. Does he look better? I ask myself. Does he look worse? I focus on his face and avoid the knotted tangle of scars on the side of his head. His cheeks have a soft flush of blood but sink beneath the cheekbone. His mouth and lips are always pale. It's Ryan, I tell myself, just a sick and sleepy Ryan. I turn off the stereo and sit down.

During my first few visits, I talked to him in the hope that the sound of my voice might bring him back. I rambled on and on about the boring details of my life while I imagined little stirrings in him—the tremble of a finger, the twitch of an eyelid, the draw of a breath. All of my imaginings came to nothing. Eventually, I got sick of hearing my own voice and stopped.

Where is Ryan? What is he feeling now? What is he thinking? Beneath the paralyzed body and frozen face he might feel everything: his own helplessness, the flare and fire of angry nerves, the splintered pieces of skull still loose in his brain. Or maybe God is kind and Ryan sleeps. Mercifully unaware, he dreams of the old life and waits for the new.

I want to shout at him. Wake up, Ryan, wake up. Fight through. You can't leave me. I'm lost without you.

Maybe he needs pain. Pain could be the only thing keeping him in this world. Otherwise, he might lose himself in the deep drift of sleep and be carried away. And if he did leave this world, I'm not so sure that he'd go to a better place.

After the nurses kick me out, I return to the hotel. I listen to the long, steady swirl of the ceiling fan until my own sleep mercifully comes. In the morning I go to church. I lay my sins on the altar and pray for Ryan.

Live by the sword, die by the sword. That's what my father said as soon as he heard the news. He spoke the words with certainty, sadness, and condemnation. Who was he to judge?

Who was he to give some kind of righteous sanction to what happened on that terrible night?

Ryan was violent. I can't deny that. Though he rarely looked for fights, he could never back down when they came his way. Too much pride and anger, I guess. He was raised with violence and he never escaped it. I'm not sure he wanted to.

But Ryan was the best friend I ever had, the most loyal and intense person I ever knew. I won't give up on him.

On a chilly fall morning I kicked back at a table outside a downtown coffeeshop. I skimmed the newspaper, finished my coffee, and lit a cigarette. Sleepy, my eyes wandered. They stared into the street, blurring with the steady flow of pedestrians and the silver streaking of traffic.

As I stared, a black-apronned woman leaned over my shoulder. Her right hand held a cigarette while her left hand ran a wet cloth over my table. Her sleeve slipped open and I saw an orange and silver butterfly on her wrist.

I looked up. She was thin, sickly thin. Her long fingers looked no thicker than the cigarette she held.

"Hope?"

The woman finished wiping the table. She brushed a dark tangle of hair out of her eyes and glanced at me. "Hi, John."

"What are you doing here?"

"Just working," she said.

I hugged her. She hung limp in my arms. I felt the sharp bones of her shoulders poke against her shirt.

"I can't believe you're here," I said.

"I saw you before," she said. "Last week, I think."

"Why didn't you talk to me?"

She gave me an odd half-smile then tapped her ash.

"Sit down," I said, pulling the chair out for her. "How are you? How was Europe?"

She put her hand on back of the chair, but didn't sit down. "Europe was strange," she said. "It was beautiful and strange and terrible."

"What happened?"

She shrugged her bony shoulders. The gesture seemed to tire her. She brushed hair from her eyes and stared into the street. "What about you, John? Are you still on a quest for athletic glory?"

"No, my athlete days are over. I haven't played baseball since college."

Hope looked at me with disbelief. "I always thought you'd make it," she said. "I thought I'd see you on a billboard someday."

"Never happened," I said. "I guess you were right. Nothing gold can stay."

Hope dropped her cigarette to the ground. "I've got to get back to work," she said. "It was good to see you."

For the next few days, I couldn't stop thinking about her. I wondered what had happened to her and the band in Europe. The old memories returned. I remembered the nights she played and sang for me in her apartment. I remembered the power of her music, the way it melted the hours, the way it stirred and wakened my mind. Her voice travelled to me across the long years as sharp and sweet as ever. I saw her standing alone in the snowy shadows outside the bar, alone on the night she needed someone most.

I showed up at the coffeeshop on a Saturday night around closing time. She smiled when she saw me waiting for her.

"Don't you have anything better to do?" she said.

"Not really," I said. "You want a ride home?"

"No, but you can walk with me. I only live a block away."

We walked up the street together. I told her about my job, my apartment, my dog. She nodded as she listened. She walked cautiously. With each step, she grimaced and bit her lip. She pressed her weight carefully into her legs as if all of her joints were continually slipping out of place.

"Are you alright?" I said.

"Rough day."

We turned into an alley. Hope walked past the back of a few restaurants then stopped at a dumpster. When I saw two grimy faces emerge from the shadows, I jumped in front of her.

"It's alright, John," she said, pushing me back. "This is Evan and Shawna."

Hope held out a coffee and newspaper. Shawna took the coffee. Evan grabbed the newspaper.

"You guys alright?" Hope said.

Shawna nodded and sipped the coffee. She held her face over the steam until little drops of dirt and water formed on her cheeks. "Winter's coming," she said.

"I'll bring you another blanket tonight," Hope said. "You alright, Evan?"

Evan was already down on the ground crumpling newspaper pages and stuffing them under his shirt. "I'm surviving," he said.

"I'll be back in a little bit," Hope said.

We walked past the back of a bar then turned into another alley.

"Are they winos?" I asked, glancing back.

Hope stopped walking. She closed her eyes, grimaced, and pressed her hands into her hip. After a dull popping sound, she kept on. "They're homeless."

"Are they junkies?"

"They're homeless, John. They eat garbage. They sleep under a fucking dumpster while I cuddle up in a nice apartment."

We walked in silence until Hope stopped at the base of a rusty fire escape. She struggled up three flights then crawled through a cracked window. Inside, she lit a candle.

Nice wasn't the word that came to mind as I surveyed the apartment. Her furniture consisted of a single mattress thrown down in the middle of the only room. The bare hardwood floors were missing entire sections. The paint on the walls was cracked and peeling, the ceiling split with water damage. A stereo sat in one corner surrounded by small hills of albums, tapes, and CD's. A lone guitar leaned against a stack of books in another corner.

Hope set the candle on the floor. She laid down on the

mattress and covered her eyes with her wrist. I sat down on top of an empty crate.

"So what do you want, John?"

"Nothing."

"Are you lonely? Looking for a quick hookup?"

"No, no. Nothing like that."

Hope groaned. She rolled over and held the candle up to a half-dozen prescription bottles on the floor. She took two pills from one bottle and three from another. She found a bottle of water buried in her mound of blankets and swallowed the pills.

"Sorry," she said, laying back down. "I get nasty when my legs hurt."

Over the next ten minutes, as the pills worked their way into her system, Hope told me the story of her accident. It had happened on the pier less than a mile away. After a night of restless dreaming, she had walked to the pier to watch the sunrise. A car had jumped the curb and struck her from behind. The impact had shattered her hip, thrown out her back, broken her legs in fourteen places. The driver was a young guy working two full-time jobs to pay his child-support. He hadn't slept in two days. During a host of surgeries, the doctors filled her legs with pins, screws, and plates. They did what they could then sent her to an outpatient facility. She learned to walk again after a year of physical therapy.

"I never want to see a doctor, nurse, or needle again," she said.

"What happened to the guy that hit you?"

"He tried to kill himself before the trial."

"He didn't succeed?"

"No, his mom found him in time."

"That's too bad."

"Don't say that. He already hates himself. His life is shit now."

I lit a cigarette in the candle. "So how much time did he get?"

"Three years."

I shook my head. "That's nothing."

Hope started to say something, but lost the strength. Her head slipped back as the medication sunk deep into her system.

I listened to her short, weak breaths until my cigarette burned out. I kissed her hair and pulled the blankets over her shoulders.

As I turned to go, she grabbed my arm. "I forgot," she said. "Take some blankets to Evan and Shawna."

"It's freezing in here, Hope. You better keep them."

She handed me two blankets. "It's colder out there," she said. "Take them some cigarettes, too."

A few nights later we went for a walk on the beach. We sat on the rocks and watched the last red rays of the sun burn out on the choppy, grey ocean. I told Hope about Ryan. She listened in silence, her head sinking with the setting of the sun.

A hundred yards down the beach, some high-school kids drove up in jeeps and trucks. They threw wooden pallets into a pile and lit a bonfire. They pounded beers, gave warcries, and threw their bottles into the ocean. The guys ripped off their shirts. They lifted the girls onto their shoulders and threw them in the water.

"Were we ever like that?" I said.

"Probably," Hope said. She ran her fingers around the rim of a shell. "Ryan hated me, didn't he?"

"No, no. He didn't hate you."

"It's alright, John, I understand. You were all he had after he lost his father."

"He didn't hate you, Hope. Not after he heard you sing."

A smile crossed Hope's face as she stared into the fire. She rubbed her hip, leaned down, and dropped the shell in the sand. When her head lifted, the smile was gone. "That was the worst night of my life," she said.

"It was the crowd," I said. "They just wanted to dance and get drunk."

"That's all most crowds want."

"Was Europe any better?"

She shrugged. "They loved us when we played what they wanted to hear."

"Did your band get a contract?"

She nodded and brushed the hair from her eyes. "We made three CDs altogether."

"I have to hear them."

"No, you don't."

"I want to."

"Please don't ever listen to them, John. Please. I'm asking you as a friend. They're not what you're imagining."

"They can't be that bad."

"They are. The first was experimental and disjointed. The second was stock and formula. The third was fraudulent."

"You're exaggerating."

"We lost our way, John. Our music turned to ash in our hands."

"Was it the money?"

"Not really," she said. "Everyone chose their own suicide. David lost his soul slowly. He sweat it out in the arms and bedrooms of a hundred strangers. Eric turned hard. He became arrogant and stupid. His guitar-playing became public masturbation. Clint kept his heart but lost his mind. He dropped acid as often as I lit cigarettes."

"And what about you?"

"Me? I turned dead inside and tried to fake it. I spewed bullshit onto the page and into the microphone."

"Don't talk like that, Hope."

Hope stared into the ocean, her eyes a wet sliver. "What's done is done," she said. "The best I can do now is face the ugly truth."

"You haven't quit singing, have you?"

"My voice is gone. I traded it away for a mountain of cigarettes."

"You sound fine."

"I sound like gravel."

I picked up the shell and threw it into the ocean. "Even if everything you say is true, Hope, you still have your honesty."

"My honesty is exactly what I lost."

I found the band's CDs at a small music store near the pier. I listened to all three on the way to visit Ryan.

Midway through the first CD, *always dying, never dead*, I knew that Hope had been too critical. The music was experimental, maybe even disjointed at times, but a certain rawness and spontaneity held it together. There were two-minute songs and ten-minute songs. There was strong guitar and drums, but also harmonica, piano, and violin. Hope tested her voice with different styles and ranges. Her lyrics, vivid as ever, carried me through an array of images and moods.

On the second CD, *Solomon's Winds*, I quickly noticed a studio influence. Restraint and self-consciousness had replaced spontaneity. The instruments seemed to compete rather than blend. The songs were all about four minutes in length with simple structures of bridge and chorus. There were moments of greatness, but most of the music seemed half-hearted.

I listened to three songs on *Blood and Kisses*. The first song attempted to create a futuristic sound with frenetic keyboards and mixing. The second song had meaningless lyrics and an obnoxious guitar solo. The third was an obligatory love song. I quit listening before the fourth.

After a month I asked Hope to move in with me. She gave me a thin smile. "I like my place, John."

Occasionally she spent the night at my apartment, but most of the time we hung out at hers. We kicked back on her mattress, shared cloves, and listened to music for hours. On good nights we talked past midnight. On bad nights we lay in silence and ignored each other. In the blackest hours I feared that loneliness was the only thing holding us together.

Hope lived on tea, cigarettes, and scraps of toast. I begged her to eat something solid, but she said the painkillers only worked on an empty stomach.

I watched her slip into strange rhythms of living and suffering. She didn't take the pills when the pain hit hardest. She fought the pain, cursing and moaning, curled up in her mound of blankets. When the pain subsided, she crawled out of the mound and swallowed a handful of pills. Then she waited, flat on her back. As the pills travelled into her system, the tension left her body. Her eyes glazed over. Her mouth slipped open in helpless ecstasy.

Later, she wrote.

She never showed me any of the writing. I had to sneak into her apartment when she was at work.

"Tribes" was some kind of primeval myth. On a sunless, three-mooned earth, tribes of men wandered stony hills. Ash covered their feet, clung in flakes to the sweat on their backs. Two tribes clashed where the thin streams met. The men loosed their beasts to battle. Black-horned, armored with silver spikes and scales, the beasts charged forth. The champions fought over earth and stream. The battle ended when one beast gored the belly of the other. The triumphant tribe followed their champion into the hills. The losing tribe drowned their wounded beast in the stream then scattered in shame.

After the first few readings, I thought "bluesandsky" was a simple poem about love and longing. The surface was deceptively clear and smooth, the places so easy to find and feel. I lost myself in the slide of fingers on my neck, the warm and golden sun, the crumble of sand, the wide and heavy blue above me. But over time and after many readings, the voice changed. The young and pleading voice turned colder. I realized that her search for love was really a search for truth. In the end, she found the truth but left her love behind. When I finally understood the last line, I found myself at the edge of a desert rather than an ocean.

"Of the Last" was a mystery I could never solve. It repelled analysis and refused dissection. The deeper places opened only for the free of mind and pure of heart. Even then the path remained elusive.

Love was the first thing I stole

legions wait in the dust of the hill, pleading for

an end to mercy
sky and earth, nothing can rise, nothing will fall
let the killers come

faces above her she hears, feels, the blankets sweat, the bed,
the depths below her, touching, licking, calling
rage boils the seas, shakes the bones of Ahab
sleep is coming

shadowed and thick, what hides behind the grey?
she watches the child,
her falling,
her fading

burn, burn, heal and burn
never wanted to see this far

Remember me when you get home.

The mystery remained. I thought it might be solved if I heard Hope put the words into music.

She wouldn't sing for me so I looked around and bought some recording equipment. I told her that my friend from work was moving and couldn't take the equipment with him.

"You're lying," she said.

I shrugged. "Do you want me to throw it all away?"

She pulled the amp from the first box. She touched each of the knobs, circling them with her finger. She opened the second box.

The call came in the middle of the workday. I stared into the ocean for an hour before calling Hope.

"What's wrong, John?"

"Ryan's fading," I said.

She mumbled something. I heard her light a cigarette and exhale.

"I know you hate hospitals," I said, "but I need you to go with me."

Neither of us talked. Hope rested her head against the windshield and watched the hayfields brush by. I stared down the broken line in the center of the road. I watched the line swerve and bend with the sway of the hills.

When we got into town, we shared a cigarette in the parking lot of the convalescent center.

"Are you scared?" she asked.

"I'm scared. I'm tired. I'm numb."

"Maybe he'll pull through this," she said. "Maybe he'll even wake up. You never know."

A lightness entered my chest. I imagined Ryan waking, rising, putting his bare feet onto the floor, looking around the room with a confused grin.

"He's not coming back," I said. "This is goodbye."

The doctor met us at the front desk. I shook his hand then trudged down the hall. Hope stayed to ask him a few questions.

As I entered Ryan's room, I noticed a few pieces of new equipment around his bed. I settled into my usual chair, kicked out my feet, and exhaled a roadweary breath. I stared at the floor until the tiles blurred.

Before I could drift off to sleep, the doorhandle turned. I heard footsteps. I wanted to lift my head, but the lure of sleep sweetly called. I felt the heaviness of my limbs as I hung between rest and waking. The footsteps stopped. With a soft groan, I lifted my head and looked up.

In an instant I knew that something incredible had happened. Hope stood close to the bed, her knees brushing the white and blue blankets. She stared down at Ryan. Her legs were still crooked and unnatural. Her sharp bones still poked against her skin. Her long hair still hung in her eyes. But something had changed in her. The bitterness was gone from her eyes. The self-hatred, too.

Her mouth hung open. Her hands shook. Her chest lifted with heaving breath.

As she stared down at Ryan's prone body, I wondered what it was that gripped her. Did she realize that her own days in the hospital, terrible as they were, could have ended worse? Maybe she saw time. She saw the years that Ryan had lost, the years that she and I had been given, the years we still had left. Maybe she was simply stricken with Ryan's helplessness, the lifelessness of someone she remembered so vividly alive.

Whatever it was, she walked to Ryan's bed and took his face into her hands. She kissed him. She held her lips against his cheek. She rested her forehead against his tangle of scars. In that single gesture I found beauty in the midst of death, meaning among the wreckage and scars of violence, God in a godless world. All the long and bitter threads of my life ceased their writhing and burning as they were bound by the power of that single act of love.

She sat down in a chair next to me. Drained of color and emotion, she closed her eyes.

"This is it," I said.

She nodded.

"Tonight's all we have," I said.

She rested her head against the wall. Clenching her jaw, she shifted her legs into the least painful position she could find.

I stared at Ryan. I noticed a fork of purple veins on his forearm. His nose hung in the air, alone above the rest of his face. His hair had grown thick but still couldn't cover his large ears.

"I wish you could have seen him when he was young," I said. "Really young. Sixteen, seventeen, eighteen. When you're both a boy and a man. Ryan was something back then. Everybody's wild when they're young, but Ryan was something else. He was fearless." I glanced at Hope. "Are you awake?"

"Keep talking," she said, her eyes closed.

"I don't know. Maybe it wasn't the purest feeling in the world, but when we were together I felt invincible. When I was with Ryan, I felt like I could do anything."

I walked over to the machines. I listened to their regulated humming and watched the soundless blinking of their lights.

"Keep talking, John."

"There's nothing more to say."

"Tell me stories."

"You know all the stories," I said. I left the machines and sat back down. "I just wish he'd had a little more time. Just a year or two. He could have pulled out of the tailspin, you know. He could have found his way."

"He would have."

"I don't know which memories to trust," I said, "which Ryan to remember. Do I remember him in the sunlight, smiling, happy, strong, or do I see him in the night, ready to kill someone?"

"Just love him," she said. "That's all you can do."

We sat in silence.

After Hope dozed off, I moved my chair next to Ryan's bed. I took his hand and pressed it between my own.

An hour before dawn the warmth left his hand.

Three days later we laid his body in the earth.

I drifted. During the long, grey days I stared out of my office window into the ocean. During the long nights I stared at the shadows of my bedroom walls. I spent weekends with Hope, but we slept more than we talked. Hope's mind slipped in and out of clarity within her shifting cloud of pain and pills.

One morning at work the receptionist called. "You have a visitor, John."

"Who is it?"

"Mr. Evans."

"Who?"

"Mr. Evans. He didn't give his first name."

"Is he a salesman?"

"No, I don't think so. He said it's personal."

I threw down my notebook and headed up the hall. In the elevator I remembered two Evans that I had known in the past: Tony Evans, a skinny outfielder on my middle-school baseball team, and Spencer Evans, an old guy in my parents' church that suffered from multiple sclerosis. I hadn't seen Tony since high-school and Spencer, if even alive, would have been pushing ninety.

When I entered the reception area, I realized immediately that neither Tony nor Spencer Evans had come to see me. I walked over to the giant man standing against the wall. We faced each other, hands at our sides.

"What do you want?" I said.

His mouth opened then closed. He took a half-step backward. "I read the notice in the paper," he said. "My friend told me you worked here. I just wanted to pay my respects, you know, see how you were doing."

"Are you kidding? Did you want to shoot some pool, smoke some cigars, get caught up?"

"No, it's not like that. I just wanted..." His voice trailed off as his courage failed him. He grimaced and looked away.

David Evans had gained a lot of weight since the trial. He had lost most of his hair, too. His rounded arms and sagging chest appeared incapable of the power and ferocity that I remembered from that dark night ten years ago.

"Come on," I said. "Let's get a drink."

We walked up the street to an Italian restaurant and ordered two beers from the bar. When the beers came, David stopped me before I could retrieve my wallet. "Please," he said. He paid for both beers and handed me my glass. We walked outside to the patio and sat down at an empty table.

"I'm sorry about your friend, John."

"His name was Ryan."

"I'm sorry about Ryan. I'm really, truly sorry. I don't know what else I can say."

I sipped my beer and shrugged. "There's nothing anyone can do now."

"If I could change what happened that night, I would. Believe me, I'd give anything to change it."

"You can't."

His tone toughened slightly. "It was an accident. I didn't know the chair was there."

"And you slipped on the floor, right?"

"The floor was slick as hell that night. I was just trying to pull Ryan out of the fight."

"No, you were pissed because you took an elbow to the jaw."

"I was just trying to pull him out of the fight. The floor was slick. I didn't mean to hurt him."

"I saw your eyes. You were pissed."

"I was pissed, but I didn't mean to hurt him. I didn't know the chair was there."

"I don't believe you," I said. "I want you to tell me man-to-man, face-to-face, that you really slipped on that floor. Forget the courts, forget the lawyers, forget the judge. Tell me man-to-man that you actually slipped on that floor."

"I swear to God, John. I didn't know the chair was there."

"Did you slip? Did Ryan's head crash into the chair because you slipped on the floor? Yes or no?"

"I don't know. We both ended up on the ground. I was pissed, I can't deny that. But I swear to God I didn't know the chair was there. I wouldn't have slammed him if I had."

"So you tried to slam him to the ground, not just wrap him up?"

He closed his eyes for a second, inhaled, then blew out an agonized breath. "Yeah. I think I did."

I shook my head. I walked to the railing and lit a cigarette.

As the traffic flowed by, I shook with grief and anger. All the helplessness that I had felt for the last ten years stirred inside me and transformed itself into a blinding rage. The rage grew as I remembered hundreds of hours spent at Ryan's bedside. Ryan never walked away from the bar that night. David Evans did. Ryan spent ten years paralyzed. No five-minute apology can make up for that.

David came to the railing and lit his own cigarette. "You don't remember, do you?"

"Remember what?"

"The ride to the hospital."

"What are you talking about?"

"We rode to the hospital together that night. You and me. Together in my car. You don't remember, do you?"

I shook my head, but I could already feel the images

stirring, rising from the depths. Like razors through flesh, they passed in my mind. I saw David's blood-spotted neck, his hand shaking on the steering wheel, the red and blue lights strobing the car's interior.

"I told you it was an accident and you believed me," David said.

I clutched the railing.

"I know you were drunk that night, John, but you believed me. You said to forget about it. You said that Ryan had started the fight."

I raised my hand a few inches from the railing. David stopped.

I stared at the tip of my cigarette. I wanted to grind the flame into my forehead. I tossed the butt into the street, knelt, closed my eyes, and pressed my head to the railing.

Who can bear the full truth? Who can suffer it? Who can withstand its searing light? I can't. With my cheek to the cold metal, I prayed for God to take away the light and the pain. I prayed to die.

But God denied me. Instead of relief, I felt a deeper, more painful truth driven into my heart. If I didn't forgive David, all my prayers for Ryan deserved to go unanswered. We were all young back then. We were all young and foolish and fragile.

I stood up from the railing and shook David's hand.

I drove into the night. I left the city and drove deep into the countryside. On the dark country highways, I stared into the bright headlights of trucks loaded with hay and corn and alfalfa. As the earth-shaking trucks got close, I squeezed the steering wheel and thought how easy it would be. One quick turn and I could finally rest.

I drove deeper into the country. The paved roads turned to dirt and gravel.

I parked alongside an irrigation canal and listened to the cool murmur of the flowing water. I heard frogs and coyotes and crickets. A breeze filled my car with the smell of freshly cut hay.

Near midnight I turned for home.

I found Hope bundled up on my couch. Kneeling beside her, I began to talk. I told her that we couldn't go on living like this. I told her that she was going to make music again. I told her that I was going to coach baseball and teach kids to love the game.

When I realized she was still sleeping, still wrapped in her medicated cloud, I stopped talking. I laid down in the middle of the floor, offered God a weary prayer, and drifted away in the whir of the ceiling fan.

Thanks

God

Hope Sandoval and Mazzy Star

Zach, Che, Zapata, and Subcomandante Marcos

Solzhenitsyn, SE Hinton, Cervantes, and Dostoyevsky

Renzo Gracie, Vitor Belfort, Heath Herring, and Dajiro Matsui

Mom, Dad, Damaris, Michael, Bill, Eric, Dustin, Christina, Sarah, George, Dawn, Peggy, Marie, Mrs. Rhode, and Corrie.

William English

David Shord